THE OTHERS

(TESSA EXTRA-SENSORY AGENT BOOK 2)

KFIR LUZZATTO

PINE 10

CONTENTS

COPYRIGHT NOTICE

CHAPTER 1

I had to keep myself from reading Mary's mind. She had said that I should only read her in an emergency, but she had kept me waiting for more than 15 minutes, which to me, qualified as an emergency. I hate waiting.

Who is Mary, you ask? Well, I can't help it if you haven't been paying attention to what has been going on with me. I'll fill you in, but I don't like to repeat myself, so pay attention from now on. Mary is my new boss, who replaced someone who had tried to kill me and ended up with his head smashed into a pulp. That happened because I got exposed to a gadget that fiddled with my brain waves and unleashed my innate extra-sensory ability. You never know what goes on inside your box until someone messes around with it.

Mary's official title was Undersecretary for Something or Other, but for real, when this story began, she was managing the ESA operation. "ESA" stands for Extra-Sensory Agency. Simply put, she was in charge of all the weirdos, including myself, who had developed unusual abilities one way or another. My unique ability is telepathy—I can read your mind, but I can also actually take over its management altogether. I know what I'm saying—I can control you, and I can't help it if it sounds spooky, but that's one of my skills, and for me, it's pretty fun. Not so much for the bad guys who have the misfortune of getting on my wrong side.

Oh, and I almost forgot to say that I saved Mary's life. Twice, so she owes me big time, although she tends to forget that. It looked like she forgot this time. Listen to what mission she had cooked up for me and judge for yourself.

It was the first time I had seen her new posh office into which she had moved only recently, and it was impressive. It had a big desk, a luxurious sitting area, and a large window with a park view. Her secretary ushered me in, and Mary greeted me with a broad smile.

"Hi, Tessa. Sorry to keep you waiting," she said.

She patted the leather coach's cushion on which she was sitting, inviting me to come and sit beside her.

"Wow! They are treating you well. This is a cool office."

"Yes, it comes with the territory. They reward a good job around here, pretty much as we rewarded you."

I can't say that she was wrong. The apartment where Liv and I stayed and the government was paying for, was cozy and well-furnished. We had no complaints. I told you about Liv, didn't I? Lieutenant Liv Ellman is my BFF, and, so you know, we are; how should I put it ... more than mere friends. She's not just a pretty face—and pretty all over, at that—but also a brain scientist and currently in charge of my brain's health—but I will get to that later.

"Alrighty, what's up?" I asked.

"I have wonderful news for you; you're going back to school."

I had to say those words back to myself in my head to believe she had spoken them.

"What? Are you crazy?"

Cheeky, right? But that's me—I say it as I see it. I haven't attended a proper school since I was 14, but the government trained me well during basic training and beyond. True, the curriculum wasn't exactly the same as you get when you go to an average high school because it was personalized. I learned a lot of math, physics, and geography (which I hated), and I read a lot because I apparently needed a broad education. I read even more than required simply because I like reading. Properly speaking, I am a bookworm. One thing I knew for sure: I definitely did not need any more schooling.

"No, listen: this is not about you; it's for a mission," Mary hastened to explain.

"Good! You had me scared for a moment. What's this mission about?"

"It's a rather long story. Let's start by saying that the government operates a research center near Emendale. That's a small town, so small that it's difficult to find it on the map. This research center officially develops agricultural and environmental solutions. But in fact, it's a high-security facility that employs our best brains."

"So, what do they develop there?"

"It doesn't matter; you don't need to know. The place is so secret that people in one department don't know the scientists who work in the others. There are four distinct departments, each with its separate building, access, and facilities. We are concentrating here on two of those scientists. The first one is Doctor Joseph Burns, who specializes in honeybees."

"Honeybees? That sounds dangerous," I said and laughed.

Mary gave me a severe look and continued.

"As I said, we concentrate on two scientists. The second one is Doctor Abraham Aiken, whose specialty is wild wheat."

"Wild? That's even more dangerous than honeybees— sorry," I said when I saw a pained look on Mary's face, "I'll try to stay serious, but you're making it hard for me."

"Good. Be quiet and listen. As I said, the work they do at the research center is top secret. They have no work relations with each other, and that's done on purpose. Nobody can guess what that project is or where it's going without having all the pieces of the puzzle. So imagine how worried we were when we discovered a leak; information available only to those two scientists who work in different departments had been obtained by a non-authorized individual."

"So, these two doctors are leaking information, right?"

"A different agency branch raised the alarm, and that's what they initially thought. But after a thorough investigation, they concluded this was not the case. How they reached that conclusion is too complicated to explain, and there's no need to go through all of it. Simply put, the leaked information consisted of snippets only available to the scientists. But here's the punchline: those snippets were incomplete to the extent that the information was useless. There is a rumor that circulates in Emendale about the research that is going on there. The rumor as a whole is utterly absurd, but some of the details are true and could not be known without having access to those two scientists and their work. We couldn't find the source of the rumor but concluded that the scientists were not leaking and that whoever acquired that information had taken it at random and not skillfully. So we came up with a hypothesis about how this information had leaked."

"A telepath!" I was excited. That meant that there were others like me out there. True, I had not invented telepathy, but all the others I had heard of until now had very minimal capabilities. None of them would be able to dig into the minds of a couple of scientists to extract top-secret information. Except for Bill, of course, but he was dead. I'll tell you about Bill in a minute.

"Spot on! That's the only explanation that we have so far. It puzzled us for a while, and we wondered why those two particular scientists were involved, so we looked for similarities. The only point of contact we found was that they both have sons in high school, each a seventeen-year-old like you—"

"I'm barely that, and for your information, I look younger!"

I like to keep the record straight. Mary gave me a poisonous look and went on without acknowledging the interruption.

"Doctor Burns' daughter, Jenny, and Doctor Aiken's son, Jim, are in the same class. So the theory, right now, is that someone who knows them and moves in their social circle is a telepath and is the one who obtained and leaked the information. So we are looking for a teenager telepath."

"That makes sense. So what's the plan?"

"We want you to go there and ferret out that telepath for us. You were so good at that last time, and we know we can count on you."

"It takes one to find one, right? So how am I going to do that?"

"The school year starts in two weeks. Congratulations, you are enrolled in Emendale High. Get ready for orientation week."

CHAPTER 2

L et me tell you about Bill. He was a nice, kind old man who lived in a small apartment alone with a dog. When I got to know him, we really bonded, and the fact that he was a telepath made the bond instantaneous and strong.

It all started the week after Mary got promoted to manage the ESA operation. I thought the job would go to ESA15, aka "The Director," but no—he had continued managing the organization's research center, where everything had begun. I'll tell you a bit more about it later. Anyway, Mary called me to the unit's laboratory—a super-high-tech setup. You acceded to it via a dilapidated, old building with a "Spare Parts Storage" sign that meant nothing and drew no attention from anybody. Liv was also at the lab.

"What was so urgent to make me run here?" I asked.

"Something has come up that we need your help with. Look at this machine," Mary said, pointing to what I had thought was a coffeemaker.

"What is it, an espresso machine?"

"No, it's an MWR. Liv will explain."

"MWR stands for Mixed Waves Receiver. You remember the MWA, the Mixed Waves Amplifier that started everything," Liv explained. "While the MWA can amplify the brain waves that induce telepathy, the MWR can detect when someone is using telepathy because it detects the amplified mixed waves."

"How do you know that it works?"

"It turns out that while you were training, back at the base, Doctor Alexander, the scientist who developed the MWA, was working on it."

I don't think I told you about "the base" to which she was referring. That was a top-secret site where civilians, aided by the military, developed all kinds of unconventional stuff. That was where putting me into the MWA machine changed my brain wiring and made me a much better and stronger telepath than I originally was.

"May he be burning in hell," I interjected. I had disliked the man, who was part of a plot to get me killed, once I was no longer useful to a certain project. The fact that he had got himself killed in the process had done nothing to make me like him any better.

"He probably is," said Mary with a smile, "but listen to the end."

"As I was saying, Doctor Alexander was a compulsive inventor, and while you trained, he developed the MWR and tested it on you without your knowing it. We found a very basic prototype," said Liv, patting the coffeemaker-like thing, "and we recovered his notes from his computer as well."

"So, what does the machine do?"

"Not much. It can alert us when a high level of mixed waves is present but is not very location-specific. It cannot pinpoint the origin of the phenomenon, but only a very approximate location."

"I see. So why are we wasting time on it?"

"Well," said Mary, looking hesitant, "first of all, we want you to be aware of these things because just like we have such a machine, bad agents—foreign agents—might develop one. We also found something else in Doctor Alexander's papers: a project for a shield. He didn't make a prototype, but it's a rather simple thing to make, and we will want to test it with you as soon as we have built one."

"What is a 'shield'?"

"It's a device that, if Doctor Alexander was right, can prevent a telepath from reading you. As long as you keep it on, it protects you from unwanted reading. The prototype that Doctor Alexander had planned is not a very practical thing to use because it is heavy and bulky. We will eventually miniaturize it to make it possible to carry it concealed. It will take a lot of work and no little money, but it is doable."

"Well, thank you for all the information. Are we done here?"

"Not quite," said Mary. "We have taken the MWR for a ride, and, to our astonishment, it started to beep in several different areas."

"Wow! So you found other telepaths?"

"Well, not yet, but we would very much like to find them. If we can convince whoever they are to come and work for us as you do, that would be a great addition to our unit."

"From what you are saying, telepathy is much more common than we thought."

"That seems to be true, but it also seems that many telepaths are weak or only sporadically active, and perhaps they even don't know that they are telepaths. Certainly, the signals we detected would seem to indicate that this is the fact—with one exception," Liv explained.

"What exception?"

"We detected one signal that was both strong and continuous. That indicates an active telepath using his or her gift consciously."

"Good, so?"

"So we want you to find him or her for us," Mary concluded.

Finding Bill wasn't that difficult, and they could have done it without me using their machine, but it was kind of fun ferreting him out. The device had narrowed the location to a small apartment building, so I started by sitting outside mid-morning and opening my mind to whatever happened there. I heard a lot of uninteresting chatter, but by then, I was trained so well that I had learned to shut out "voices" that didn't interest me. That proved to be a great way to go by elimination, and at the end of the second day, I had narrowed it down to five or six potential voices.

On the third day, I was sitting outside on a bench, my mind open to the voices coming from the building, when something caught my interest. It was an unusual thought: *I'll take you for a walk in a minute. Let me finish my coffee; be a good dog!* It was strange because that's something you may tell a dog, but you don't think it "out loud." Ten minutes later, I saw a man, about sixty years old, walking out of the building with a dog—a mongrel—on a leash. The leash was slack, and they walked toward a nearby park. I decided to follow.

Watching the man and the dog strolling was fascinating. They walked so much in unison that it seemed like they were talking. I got a little closer and listened in. *Let's sit here for a minute* was the thought that reached me, and the dog turned toward a close-by bench without being pulled and sat beside it. It was awesome! True, I had tried reading a cow and failed, and I never managed to communicate a thought directly to somebody's mind, but apparently, it could be done. I expect that dogs are brighter than cows and perhaps much more human, too.

I sat on the bench beside him and smiled at him. He gazed back at me, looking surprised by my presence.

"Hi! I'm Tessa," I said.

He smiled back. He had a pleasant, fatherly smile, and I instinctively and immediately liked him.

"Hello. What can I do for you?"

"You can teach me to talk to your dog like you do."

"What do you mean?" He furrowed his brow, and the smile disappeared.

"You know what I mean: with your mind."

Up to that point, I had not given away anything, and if it turned out that I was wrong and he was no telepath, no harm would be done. He would think that I don't have all my marbles, and that would be it. But he decided to test me to see if he had to come clean.

If you can read what I'm thinking, tell me that now, he thought.

"Yes, I can read what you're thinking," I said, and I saw the tension leaving him.

"Thank God! I thought I was the only one," he said at last.

We went into a long, emotional discussion that lasted two hours or more, using our thoughts and words. He told me about himself, his life—he had retired from an unimportant office job. His joy at being able to communicate with his dog on an intimate level felt kind of contagious. We sat on that bench, forgetting the time, lost in our own world. I had never talked to another telepath. For the first time in my life, I realized what level of closeness you reach when you use more than one communication channel.

"Time for me to go back. My friend's lunchtime is well over-due, and he's starting to get restless," he said at last.

"But there's so much more that I want to ask you! I'm not done asking," I complained.

"Come see me tonight, and we can talk as much as you want," he said.

That evening I went to see him. I was all aflutter. I can't explain why. It felt like the world was different, that I was not a weirdo; that ordinary, simple, everyday people were telepaths too; that it was a "normal" thing to be. Bill had made coffee and heated a cake, and we sat at the kitchen table like ordinary people talking about everyday things.

"Can I talk to your dog?" I asked.

"You can try, but I don't know if he'll connect with you. He's been my faithful friend for five years, and only one year ago, I managed to make contact with him. Sometimes dogs are more reserved than people."

"I'll try."

I closed my eyes and thought about the dog. I tried hard to get through to it, but nothing came. I opened my eyes and gazed straight at it. The dog raised its head and shook it as if to say "no," so I let it go.

That evening was both enlightening and exhausting. We conversed, mixing words and thoughts until I felt drained by the intensive telepathic connection. Bill answered so many of my questions with patience, skirting no subject, that I ended up feeling a real kinship with him.

"I'm exhausted," I said at last. "I learned so much, and I have so much more to ask, but I think I should go now and catch some sleep."

"I'm a bit tired too," said Bill, "but I'm glad we did this. You are a remarkable young woman. Take some cake with you—for the road."

Arguing that I lived nearby didn't get me anywhere, so I took a generous slice of cake and left. We agreed to meet again in the park the next day and continue our talk.

The next day, I waited for Bill on the same bench where we had met the morning before. He arrived with his dog, and again, I couldn't help admiring the perfect communion of man and dog. It was evident in every movement and how they looked at one another. It was a natural continuation of our previous evening, and we kept talking about many things—parents, friends, the scent of spring, pizza—but this time using telepathy only. I listened to him, and he listened to me, and somehow, the conversation flowed. I had meant to talk to him about Mary and the job, but somehow I couldn't bring myself to kill the magic with business talks. I had no idea how he would react after learning what kind of work I was doing. *I'll talk to him about Mary tomorrow,* I decided.

"I have to go home early today," said Bill. "I have an electricity inspector coming—some issues with the building, a nuisance. Let's talk again tomorrow."

I nodded, and he got up at the same time as his dog. They started walking toward the street that ran beside the park, toward their apartment building. I remained sitting on the bench, thinking about all the new things I had heard from him. I was lost in a reverie when brakes' screeching sound and a loud thud brought me back to the present. I saw a black van stopping for a second where a moment before Bill and his dog were crossing the street, and then it sped away. I tried to read its number plate, but it was too dirty and too far. It took me a second to realize that there would be no more chats with Bill. He and his dog lay on the street in a pool of blood in what looked like a loving embrace.

I brag that I never cry, which is not true; although I haven't cried for years, all I could do was sit on the grass and weep.

Mary got angry at me. I had never seen her so sore, and all simply because I had suggested that there was something fishy about the accident. Bill had been killed by a hit-and-run vehicle with smudged license plates, and it looked too much like a professional hit job. Maybe I was being paranoid, but the burnt child ...

"You disobeyed orders, and instead of bringing him to us, you played games with his dog. This is unconscionable conduct!"

"But Mary—"

"Don't 'but Mary' me! I had already obtained the resources needed to recruit another telepath, and you blew it! You can consider yourself responsible for what happened!"

That stung. I already felt unreasonably responsible for Bill's death, but she shouldn't have said that.

"But what if it wasn't an accident?"

"How? Why? Why would someone be interested in killing a retired old man? Don't be stupid. Now go!"

There was something in what Mary said—Bill was a nobody, and if someone wanted to kill him, it wasn't because of me. It had to be an accident unless Bill had been targeted because of something he had done before I met him. Be as it may, he had taken his secret to the grave. There was no point in beating myself up about it. I had no way of knowing.

CHAPTER 3

"Tessa, meet your mother and father," said Mary. "Or, rather, I should say, Alexandra, meet your mom and dad."

I looked at them and felt depressed. According to the datasheet that Mary had given me, "Dad" worked in shipping, most of the week from a home office, and "Mom" was a housewife. We were the Joneses, a happy little family of dorks. Couldn't the Service highbrows be a bit more imaginative than that? At least, this time, Mary had picked a reasonable name for me—last time, she had chosen Annabelle, can you imagine? But I could work with Alex.

"But Mary," I said, sounding less pleading than I was, "why can't Liv and Tom be my mommy and daddy? I won't feel like shooting myself in the head if I had to spend time with them."

Wait a moment; I haven't told you about Tom, have I? I had met him in Switzerland. He had been deployed there by the Secret Service to help with an operation—the one during which I had met Mary. Long story. Initially, his job was to keep an eye on me, but as things developed, he had totally become my personal agent. At one point, he had a crush on me, but later we became friends with benefits. He lived with his father ten minutes from my apartment and visited us often to take care of the benefits. When he did, Liv tactfully discovered she was backlogged on her shopping. At first, I worried that she might be jealous, but I read her mind enough to make sure that she wasn't. Besides, she too was seeing someone—not an actual boyfriend, purely a casual friend—so we were even. The Secret Service had assigned Tom to Mary's department, which was convenient for everybody concerned.

Anyway, the moment I asked Mary that question, I knew it was a dumb one.

"Who is going to believe they are old enough to be your parents?" she objected. "Liv looks almost as young as you."

"Yeah, you're right," I said, sighing.

"Okay, so now sit down with your loving parents and learn about your background and recent history. I'll leave you to that."

"Exciting," I said moodily.

She turned to go, and then she stopped and pivoted back.

"By the way, you need to talk to Liv."

"About what?"

"She'll tell you," Mary said, and this time she walked out.

Liv and I lived together and never stopped chatting, so this was a strange comment from Mary, but it would have to wait until I got home. I sighed some more and started to dig into the fake background of our lovely little family. I would be a school senior and expect to face questions about my junior year, my old school, and so on. Since I aimed to become popular and get to know as many people as possible, I couldn't avoid talking about myself; that meant I had to know my family history inside out. Mom (Barb) and Dad (Bob) turned out to be not as dull as I feared once I got to know them. They actually were seasoned operatives, and you had to admire their ability to make themselves look gray and threadbare. At least I had someone to rely on if things got rough at some point, as they tend to do when I'm around. I'm a trouble magnet through no fault of my own.

If I had to decide which of the many aspects of my work was the most maddening to me, the trophy would go to the need for absolute secrecy. Mary had made it clear that the mission was top secret and that nobody—absolutely nobody—was to know about it. That meant that I was not allowed to tell Liv or Tom either. I admit that I'm not a stickler for procedures, but there are a few rules that I abide by faithfully, and secrecy is one of them. So although it killed me to keep things from Liv, I had to. We were drinking coffee after a lovely dinner that Liv had ordered in, and the time had come for me to tell her.

"Listen," I said, and her eyes told me that she knew something was coming. Although I have permission from her to read her whenever I want—cementing our foundation of trust, she called it —I don't abuse it, so I kept our conversation strictly vocal.

"Yes?" she said, sitting up straight.

"I have to go away for a while. Mary has got a mission for me."

"For how long?"

"I don't know."

"Where?"

"I can't tell you. Top secret."

"Is it a dangerous mission?"

"I don't think so. It doesn't look like it."

"Will you be able to stay in touch?"

"Yes, by phone. And when did you turn into my mother?"

"I'm sorry ... it's just that I worry about you, you know that."

"You don't need to. Say, Mary said that I should talk to you. Any idea what she was talking about?" I asked, remembering Mary's parting words.

Liv nodded and averted her gaze.

"I got your test results. The battery of tests we did last week."

"And?"

"And there is something you need to know." She swallowed and gazed at the wall above my shoulder, which meant that she had bad news for me. "When you use telepathy, you deplete your brain of the resources it needs to keep neural activity precisely tuned."

"English, please!" I complained. I love Liv dearly, but I could throw a shoe at her when she starts talking scientific gibberish to me.

"What I mean is that the amplitude of your combined wave becomes smaller."

"And that's a bad thing why?"

"Because if you use it up too much and it reaches below its critical threshold, you will lose your telepathic power. If you do, it may not come back again because reaching the necessary level may come up against an energy barrier."

"Are you saying that I'm bound to lose my power?"

I had never thought this might happen, and I felt a chill along my spine.

"No, no! It will only happen if you use it up too much if you abuse it. The brain regenerates after you rest and gets back to its original state. But if you don't let it rest, who knows ..."

"So, tell me what to do."

"The only thing you can do is use your telepathic powers only when you must. No more overworking it for pleasure. Use it when you absolutely need to, and you'll be okay." She gazed straight at me, took my hand, and pressed it. "I didn't want to worry you—there is probably nothing for you to worry about—but I was afraid that you might overdo yourself if I didn't tell you. So, please, stop using your powers for fun."

"All right. I get it. I will use it only when necessary. I promise, don't worry."

I smiled at her to make her feel at ease. It wasn't her fault that my freakish mind had this quirk. As I did so, I saw a tear building up in the corner of her eye, which took me entirely by surprise.

"What's the matter?" I asked.

"Nothing. We were barely starting to feel normal and steady after all we've been through ... and you're leaving again."

Liv took a few quick breaths that sounded more like sobs, and all I could do was hug her.

"I'm not leaving, silly you! It's only work."

I tried to pull back and look at her, but she wouldn't let go.

"Don't speak, please. Just hold me."

"All right, but I'm not going to China or anything. I'll be virtually around the corner. Stop worrying, okay."

"Okay," Liv said, sniffing.

We remained on that couch in each other's arms until we fell asleep. When I woke up, I had a crick in my neck, but Liv was sleeping peacefully, so it had been worth it.

CHAPTER 4

Emendale is not a bad place if you are a farmer or a mortician. If you walk west of what they pompously call the "Main Street" for two blocks, you stumble on a train station that consists of a couple of dusty platforms. A tiny station building with windows that had not been washed this century, and a rusty railroad, are all that welcomes you there. There wasn't a soul around when I got there on my first day in town. To expand my horizons, I returned to Main Street and walked east for three minutes. That's all it took for me to reach the countryside, which extended as far as the eye could see. I think I counted four people I had seen in the last hour, but maybe it was only three.

I felt depressed, believe me. But then again, this was work. The residential area was not as bad, though. The houses were small and looked like toy cardboard structures, but most little lawns and gardens were well-kept, with flowers strewn around to liven up the scenery. Our house, to which I walked back from the ghost town, looked like taken straight out of *That '70s Show*. It was precisely what you would expect from a middle-class family home.

The house across the street from ours looked precisely the

same. An old man was sitting on a chair outside, and when he saw me, he called out.

"Hey, miss," he yelled. "Neighbor. Come here a moment!"

I walked up to him, and I could smell the booze even standing five paces from him. He slurred his words and was clearly drunk.

"What can I do for you, sir?" I asked politely—no sense in starting a feud with a neighbor.

"You movin' in?" he asked.

"Yes, we are."

"Tell your dad to come and see me sometime. I like to know the neighbors."

"I certainly will," I said with an ingratiating smile and turned away. I'd had all I needed of the stench of cheap liquor.

When I reached the house, "Dad" was affixing a sign to the door that said, "Welcome to The Joneses' Little Heaven." I looked at it and made a face.

"What's your problem with it?" he asked.

"Aside from making me want to puke, you mean?"

"Which means it's the perfect sign for us," he said, smiling. He pushed the door open to let me in.

"Mom" was busy at the kitchen stove and welcomed me with a broad smile.

"Hi, darling. How was your tour of the town?"

"It was enough to make me want to jump in front of a train, except that trains seem to avoid this place too. I hope we can complete our mission quickly and run away."

Barb turned all serious and lowered her voice.

"You shouldn't be talking like that. We need to behave normally and keep up appearances at all times. You never know who's listening; if you don't get completely into character, you'll slip up and give us away. You understand that, don't you?"

"Yes, *Mom*," I said, rolling my eyes. She was right, of course. I felt trapped in this nightmarish world, but at least I knew it would be over sometime. I went up to my room and turned on the music at full volume. I was going to be a good girl and behave rebelliously, in character with my teenage persona.

Orientation was scheduled for 10 AM the following day, and I showed up right on time. I had taken my time choosing what to wear—denim shorts and a flimsy knotted belly shirt. Barb had approved my choice, labeling it "sexy but not too openly slutty." As she dropped me in front of the school, I realized that, despite everything, I was a bit excited, as if I was going to school for real. The school building looked like any other, and seeing it took me back to my last year in a real school. That was the year before my life was hijacked, and I became a cat's paw in the government's hands. I had hated ESA15 for a long time for doing that to me, but I had buried the hatchet now. I had to after he was nice enough to go out of his way to stop a bad guy from getting me killed. But that's another story. "ESA" stands for Extra-Sensory Agent, by the way. I'm ESA54, but nobody calls me that.

Orientation was mainly for the freshmen's benefit, but I had to join them in the school hall since I was new. That involved listening to a lot of nonsense that Miss Wharburg, the principal, gave us at length. They have an awful lot of rules in that school, and she enjoyed explaining each one of them in excruciating detail. That took the best part of an hour, and I was looking forward to getting out when the torture came to an end, but no—her last sentence was, "Miss Jones, I'll see you in my office." Normally, I would have faked not hearing her, but I had to behave here. I dragged my feet along the corridor to the door with the "Miss A. Warburg, Principal" sign and knocked on it.

I should tell you a little about this Miss Wharburg. She was a spinster—55 years old or so, I guess—thin and dry, with skin like a plum left in the fridge for too long. Her hair was thin too, blondish sort of, faded, and barely reaching down to her neck. In short, one of the least attractive women I have ever seen. And besides, she said "um" way too much.

"Sit down, Alexandra," she said. "I wanted to welcome you to our school, but um ... there is something else we need to discuss."

I gazed at her with disinterest and waited for her to go on.

"My school ... this school has a dress code that is, um, decorous. We don't allow appearances that might appeal to, um, the prurient curiosity of men, if you know what I mean."

"Anything wrong with the way I dress?" I asked in my most innocent voice. She was squirming in her chair, obviously uncomfortable with the conversation we were having, and I was enjoying it.

"No, no, but um ... you are new, and I'm sure you are not familiar with our ways, and ..."

There she got stuck, clearly searching for something to say, so I decided to push a little.

"But, Miss Wharburg, if you think that my clothes are too provocative, please say so. I can take it."

"No, I mean, no. But um ... you understand what I'm saying."

"I hope I do."

"Well, then, I wish you a successful year with us. Welcome to Emendale High. You can always come to me for anything, but um ... senior year students are to gather on the front lawn in five minutes, so you'd better go now."

I left, not a moment too soon, and joined a small crowd of about forty on the front lawn. They were standing there, talking to each other and paying no attention to the explanations of a senior by the name of Gregg. He stood on a box that functioned as an improvised stage and was reading out a laundry list of information for those of us who wanted to listen; if you ask me, that included almost nobody. After a while, Gregg gave up and stepped down.

Another boy took his place, and by the shouts of "Dave!" and the sudden attention that the crowd paid him, I concluded that he was going to say something interesting.

"Hi, everybody!" he said. "As you know, I'm head of the welcome party committee, and tonight is the night. The party starts at nine at Nate's house. Everybody's invited—last chance to get wasted at Nate's expense before school. See you there!" he concluded among the shouts of pleasure from the crowd.

A party was exactly what I needed. I hadn't gone to a real party in ages—well, I had gone to one at the Intelligence base where I trained a couple of months back, but that didn't count. I looked forward to partying, but first, I had to learn who Nate was and find his house. I was trying to decide who to ask when I felt that somebody was watching me and turned around. I have this uncanny ability to sense when someone fixes his eyes on me, but then, many people claim to have that too. A boy stood there with a smile on his face.

"Hi," I said.

"Hi," he answered, blushing a little. "You are new." He stated it as a fact, not a question.

"I am. How insightful of you." It came out a little snarky on purpose. When you meet a new guy, it's good practice to establish who has the upper hand at the outset. And, indeed, he blushed a bit more. But he looked good. He had a good body, dark brown hair, and brown eyes to match, and he dressed tastefully, in contrast to many others who moped around the front lawn. He was only slightly taller than me, which I liked because I'm five foot three, and I hate to stretch my neck to talk to people. Overall, a guy worth talking to, I decided.

"I thought that you might need some help, you know ... to find your way around because you're new," he explained, looking defensive.

"Actually, I do. Do you know how to get to this party? Can you tell me where this Nate guy's house is?"

"I do. I should know that. I'm Nate," he said and smiled.

"I'm Alex," I said, giving him a hand to shake. "Tell me all about Nate and his house," I concluded.

One thing that bothered me was seeing a girl scowling at me or Nate as we spoke. I opened my mind to her and listened in. *You don't know who you're up against*, she was thinking, and since I wasn't up against anybody, that puzzled me. Nate was speaking, but I realized that I hadn't heard a word he had said. Apparently, he realized that, too, because he stopped and asked, "Are you here?"

"Yeah, sure I am. Why?" I said innocently.

"You looked distracted."

"No, I was wondering, who is that girl?"

"Nobody. Emily. She's Emily; why?"

"She was scowling at us."

"I guess she was planning to murder me," he said with a smile. "We used to go out last year."

"Oh ... I don't want to be in the way."

"You aren't, believe me. We're through."

"She seems classy and pretty," I objected. The last thing I wanted was to get in the middle of a lovers' tiff.

"She's both, but also snobbish and bossy. Forget her. Seeing me talking to you must have made her jealous, and she will scowl any time I talk to a girl. Not your problem."

"Surely not," I said, but I wasn't so sure. I was there to make friends, not enemies. "Now, tell me about the party."

CHAPTER 5

I had allowed Nate to come and pick me up. He had looked at me with puppy eyes, which makes me sick every time it happens, but it seemed the fastest way for me to get to know my way around. He came all smelly of something that I guess was intended to be aftershave lotion, but he wouldn't need to shave for a couple of years yet. I find it pathetic when boys try to impress me by behaving like grownups when they obviously are not. He stood by his car, assuming what I guess he thought was a nonchalant, mature posture. It occurred to me that he had no business being here if the party was at his home.

"Won't your guests miss you at your house?" I asked. "After all, you are the host."

"As long as the house is open and there is enough alcohol going around, nobody cares what I do or where I am, and I'd rather be here with you than at the party."

"You know that this is not a date, right?"

I put it bluntly to him to make sure he wasn't getting the wrong impression.

"I don't care what you call it."

"No, I mean it. I only got here yesterday, and it doesn't feel to me like I've even landed yet. I'm not open to dating anybody anytime soon."

"I'm patient."

The conversation was taking a turn I didn't like, so I dropped the subject. Nate opened the passenger door for me, and I got in. I'm no good at recognizing car brands, so I don't know what it was, but it was a luxury model. He drove in silence, and five minutes later, we reached a big house lighted like a Christmas tree. Music and voices sounded loud even outside the front door, making it clear that the party was already going strong. Nate guided me through an entrance fitted with a richly decorated door and a marbled entrance floor. He looked pleased with himself, and I guess that all this wealth made an impression on superficial girls. It left me cold, but I threw a "Nice place!" comment to give him some satisfaction. Payment for the ride, sort of.

We had reached French windows that, from a large sitting room, opened into a swimming pool area. People were talking and drinking by the pool, and a few were dancing.

"Come, I'll introduce you to a few friends."

I don't like to be treated like a trophy and showed off, so I checked his enthusiasm.

"If you don't mind, I'd prefer to do it alone. I like to get my own impression of people. Is that okay with you?"

Nate was visibly taken aback but put a good face on it. "Sure," he said, "but at least let me get you a drink. You don't want to move around without a glass in your hand."

"I'd love that," I said and smiled at him. I can fake warm smiles when I want to—I mean, I can make you think that I'm smiling at you even if you disgust me if I need to. It's one of my knacks. He smiled back, and a minute later, he returned with a glass of something. I don't know what it was, but it didn't matter. My version of "never take candy from a stranger" is "never take a drink that didn't come out of a bottle you saw being uncorked." As the old saying goes, the burned child fears the spilled milk—but that's a story for another time.

Outside by the pool, I looked around. From what I could see, pretty much everybody who had gathered in the morning on the school lawn, and a few more were there. As I stood debating my next move, a girl approached me.

"Hi!" she said, smiling invitingly.

She stood out in that crowd, with long, flaming red hair that jumped at you when paired with her green dress. The dress sported a risky cleavage, and you would have liked what that cleavage showed. Her eyes were also green, and her lips were accented by red lip gloss. *Sexy all over and openly out for the hunt,* I thought, *interesting.* She had the white complexion characteristic of redheads, and a slight redness on her exposed shoulders gave it away that she liked the sun a bit too much. Judging by her smile, she was coming in peace, so I assumed that she was not another one of Nate's neglected flames.

"Hi there," I answered, giving her a generous smile.

"Welcome. I'm Tracy, Tracy Walsh," she said, extending a hand.

I took it. It was warm and soft but firm, not limp—the kind of handshake I like.

"I'm Alex, and, as you have guessed, I'm new here."

"It's more than a guess. This is a small place, and we know everybody. It's great to meet someone new. Sometimes we tire of seeing the same faces all the time. How're you settling in?"

"Still a bit dazzled by the change from my previous place. Moving from a big city is a big step."

I would have expanded on that—after all, I had memorized my story just for that—but right then, an uproar came from the other end of the pool, and we turned to see what it was about. It looked like a drinking game was going on, and one of the two playing it was another redhead. We watched for a few seconds, and then I had to ask.

"That boy …"

"My twin brother, Jamie. Easy to guess, right?"

"Yes, quite evident."

"They've finished their stupid game. My brother is a dear, but he's boneheaded. Come, I'll introduce you to him."

Without waiting for an answer, she grabbed my hand and pulled me after her.

"Jamie!" she cried. "Meet Alex."

"Hi, Alex," he said after a moment of hesitation, during which he seemed to be trying to focus his vision. "I saw you at school today. Nice to meet you. Sorry I'm plastered, but I hope I'll remember you when the booze wears off."

"Nice to meet you too," I said, and I couldn't help smiling, this time for real, not the fake smile I gave Nate. I liked him instinctively. He had a great smile that exposed amazingly white, regular teeth and warm eyes. He looked good, not too thin but lithe and supple. Every movement he made was strangely graceful, and I caught myself checking him out a bit too much.

"I'm kidding. There's no way I can forget you. But if you'll excuse me, I'll go sit down for a while. This game was a bit extreme, and I don't think you'll take kindly to me puking on your shoes. Not a way to start a beautiful friendship," he added with sudden solemnity.

"Go and lie down, you idiot!" Tracy said. He nodded and went to lie on a poolside chaise lounge.

"Your brother is funny," I said.

"I love him, but sometimes he drives me mad," said Tracy.

"I'll go and get a drink," I said. This exchange had made me thirsty.

I went to the bar, put down the still-full glass Nate had given me, and filled a clean one with some bubbly liquid that didn't taste too strong. Then I went to sit in a dark corner beside the pool. I wanted to observe and think. I had started to attract attention, and I noticed several people gazing at me, some briefly and others at length, but I decided to ignore them. For the first time since getting to the party, I allowed myself to relax a little, and right then, I felt something.

I had limited experience with other telepaths, but the sensation I felt left no doubt in my mind: someone was trying to read me. When I read regular people, they don't know that I'm doing it, and even if they did, there is nothing they can do to stop me. We had tested that several times with Liv and other volunteers, back at the base where all this began and my ability developed. But the moment I feel an itchy sensation in my head, I know somebody is prying, and I immediately go into blocking mode. The problem with that is that whoever is trying to read me will know that something is stopping him and is likely to deduce that I'm a telepath. I have no other option, though. More so, since it all happens quickly, blocking the reading attempt comes instinctively, and I need to release the block if I want to allow it to happen. That takes time.

I was concentrating on my drink when this happened, and now I raised my gaze and looked around. The place was crowded, making it difficult to see what everybody was doing, but I thought I saw Jamie look at me pensively. It was only for a second, and then the ever-moving crowd blocked him from my view. The itching in my head had stopped, so whoever was trying to read me had given up. To my right, in the distance, I saw Nate and Emily talking or, rather, having an argument, judging by Emily's expression.

I opened my mind and tried to reach Jamie. I had his face well in mind, but the background noise was too great for me to be able to focus on him. There were too many people around, each with an overactive mind due to alcohol and other more hormonal reasons, so I gave that up. And here was Tracy again.

"Get up," she said. "Everybody's dying to meet you. Let's make the rounds."

Well, having Tracy introduce me was way better than having Nate show me off, so I got up and followed her. At one point, she grabbed my hand and pulled me through the crowd. She guided me toward two boys, who immediately stopped chatting and turned their attention to us.

"This is Alex, guys. She is new," she said.

"Welcome, Alex," they said in unison.

"Thank you," I said, not feeling very original for it. I would have added something but didn't get the chance to say more.

"We'll see you around at school," one of them managed to throw after me while Tracy dragged me away.

We stopped by a few other small groups, and Tracy repeated the introduction. The last stop was by two girls who stood a little aside at the crowd's edge and almost in the dark.

"Alex, this is Jenny, and this is Trish. Jenny and Trish meet Alex."

Trish was a busty brunette with a dark complexion and an elaborate hairdo. Jenny was a thin blonde, quite attractive in a mini and blue blouse.

"Hi, Alex. Loved the outfit you wore to school. It must've given Wharburg a heart attack," she laughed.

"Yes, I thought she was having a fit," I agreed, adding a chuckle of my own.

Trish was about to say something, but I saw her eyes moving to someone or something behind me. I turned to see who it was, but before I managed to do it, Tracy said, "Emily ..."

It's challenging to come up with the appropriate attitude when you meet someone who seems to hate your guts even before you have said a word to her. So I opted for a "Hi."

She met my greeting with a forced smile, and then she said, "I'm Emily. I think I am in your class. I wanted to get to know you ... so welcome. How are you ... I mean, do you need anything?"

"Oh, that's very sweet of you, but everybody is so welcoming. This is such a friendly town."

I couldn't understand what was going on. Was Emily checking out the competition? For a moment, I toyed with the idea of reading her, but then Liv's warning flashed before my eyes. I had to limit my readings to essentials, and this definitely was not it.

"Yes, isn't it? We want you to feel at home. Say, would you like to come shopping with me tomorrow? I can show you all the good places."

As far as I could tell from my earlier exploration, there weren't any "good places" to choose from. Still, keeping in mind that I was on a mission that involved socializing, I couldn't afford to turn down the offer. I gazed at Tracy, who was following our exchange, looking pensive.

"I'd love to, thanks!" I said, sounding as excited as I could manage.

"Then I'll pick you up at ten," she said, and with a little wave of her hand and a smile, she left. That made me wonder how come everybody knew where I was living. Neither she nor Nate had bothered asking for my address. But then, in a small town, every newcomer would surely be the center of attention.

"Emily has turned nicer than last year," Tracy commented.

"She seems very nice," I said.

"Hmm ..."

"Well, I guess I'll go home now. It has been a long day, and I'm tired. Thank you so much for all the introductions, Tracy."

"Don't mention it."

"See you around?"

"Sure," she said.

I spotted Nate coming our way from the other end of the pool area. I wasn't in the mood to talk to him, so I waited for another shift in the crowd to shield me from his view, and then I sneaked out. I judged that the walk home would take me more than twenty minutes; not a problem; I like to walk. I used the time to do some thinking about what seemed to be a more complex social setup than I had anticipated.

CHAPTER 6

Surprisingly, I had fun shopping with Emily and, for a moment, even forgot that I wasn't a high school senior for real. I limited my purchases to a pair of denim, while Emily bought pretty much everything she touched. I enjoyed trying everything on, though. By noon, we were both starved, and she took me to a lovely café for a salad. We ate and chatted, and when our plates were clean, it felt like I had to say something nice to her.

"I had fun today, thank you," I said, and I was sincere.

"Me too. We must do this again."

"Listen," I said, turning serious. I wanted to get this out of the way. "About Nate."

"What about him?"

"I'm not into him if that was bothering you."

"It didn't. Nate and I have a bumpy history; right now, we are not speaking—only yelling. But even if you are not into him, you should know he is into you. I know him well enough to see that."

"Yeah, I guess I got that vibe too, and that's why I bailed yesterday."

She gave me a side glance. "Nate can be very insistent, you know?"

"It won't do him any good," I declared, and her expression softened. "So, are we good?" I asked.

"We're good. I like you, and I like that you are direct."

"That's me. What you see is what you get," I said, and I had to suppress a smile, thinking, *what you see is so not what you get ...*

"Are you coming to the nature feast tonight?" she asked, changing the subject.

"What is the 'nature feast,' harvesting or something?"

"No, silly," she laughed. "It's our traditional party before the school year begins. We have a bonfire, music, beer, and fun."

"You party a lot," I observed. "Do you have anything more dangerous than beer there? Because I don't do drugs."

"Someone is sure to bring some grass, but nothing stronger. No Coke or things like that. We don't want the police to break it up."

"All right. So whose house is it this time?"

"No house. It's in the open, in a clearing in the woods. Do you know where the cemetery is?"

"Creepy! I saw it; it's next to a small church, right?"

"Right. Behind it is all a wooded area. You walk past the church and into the woods, and that's where we have it every year. You'll find it easily by the music and the bonfire's light. Don't come before ten, though, because that's when things start to get going. I'll be there earlier to help organize the food, so I'll see you when you arrive."

"Oh, I don't know ..."

"Don't be a party pooper! I'll wait for you."

"I'll think about it," I said. I was definitely going to go, but I didn't want to sound too eager.

We parted ways outside the café, and I walked home. I needed to consult with Dad and Mom.

"Yes, of course, you should go," said Bob, "but I want to make sure that you don't walk into anything risky. We don't know how wild these high school boys are. I'll drive you there, and I'll do a little snooping around, too, to be on the safe side."

"Hey, you're not my real father, you know?" I pointed out. I don't like being treated like a snowflake.

"Dad's right, honey," said Barb. She was better at playing the family part than Bob and me. "Let's keep in mind that we don't know who you are up against here. We can't afford to be remiss."

"Okay, all right, but please be invisible. If my schoolmates see my father snooping around, my social status will never recover."

"I will. Take this," said Bob, handing me a box. I opened it.

"I have a watch, and it's way nicer than this one."

"But your watch doesn't transmit Mayday distress signals and location data. This one will do it if you click this button three times in rapid succession. I'll feel much better staying away if I know that you're wearing it. We don't know what kind of dangers may be out there."

I realized that I was being bitchy while Bob was being a dear. He was worried about me and acting fatherly. I warmed up to him and resolved to be nicer to him—well, as nice as I can be when working.

"All right. I'll try to forget how ugly it is, and if it makes you feel better, I'll wear it."

"Good. Now let's pick your clothes for tonight," said Barb, cutting the discussion short.

That night, before leaving for the bonfire, I called Liv. It was a short and tense call for no reason. I told her I was doing okay, and she said, "Uh-huh." I told her that I missed her, and she didn't say it back, so I said that I needed to go and I would call her again soon, and she said, "Good." Something was going on with her, and I resolved to read her when I got back that night. I used to do that a lot while away in Switzerland, and it was the fastest way to find out what was on her mind—literally. Only I never got around to doing it.

Bob drove me to the side of the cemetery, where a clear path went straight into the woods. We waited in the car for a minute, listening to the music that came from somewhere behind the first line of trees. The bonfire's light created a strange illusion as if the trees were dancing, which was very much in tune with the place's spookiness. Candles in paper bags dotted the path, illuminating it enough to allow following it toward the brighter light.

"I wouldn't mind if you waited a few minutes while I checked out this party. I may want to stay or not," I said. Somehow, I wasn't sure this party was right for me—just a feeling, you know.

"Sure. I'll wait for fifteen minutes, and if I don't see you coming back by then, I'll leave. You can always call me if you want me to come to pick you up later. I'm not going to bed anytime soon. Not before I'm sure you're back and safe," said Bob.

He was being a dear again. Knowing that I had him watching out for me boosted my confidence. I nodded and got out of the car. The night was warm, so I had chosen a belly shirt above the knee-ripped jeans I particularly love. As I stood there, cold air brushed against my exposed skin, sending a shudder along my spine. It lasted only for a few seconds but combined with the creepy view of the graves on the left of the path, it made me uneasy. I tightened my grasp on my cell phone for comfort. Anybody who knows me will tell you that I'm courageous, so don't get the impression that I had turned into a timid little girl, but this was objectively spooky. Still, even if you are spooked, that doesn't mean that you turn around and run away.

I followed the path, and going past a few lines of trees, I reached the clearing in the woods where the bonfire was. They had piled up quite an impressive stack of wooden boxes, old furniture, and a mix of other wooden items, and the fire was burning high. It made crackling sounds and sent sparks sky-high. The music, which from afar had sounded loud enough, was almost deafening. It came from impressively big loudspeakers that I thought were too close to the fire to be safe. The atmosphere was one of energized partying. Little wonder since the alcohol going around was definitely stronger than beer. I saw discarded bottles of vodka, scotch, and other miscellaneous poisons. A boy and a girl I hadn't met before danced beside the fire. They moved like possessed souls, mindless of the sparks that the fire showered on them whenever a moist piece of wood spurted them out with a loud puff.

I looked around for Emily but couldn't see her anywhere, nor did I see anybody I had spoken to the night before, which made me feel like a complete outsider. I moved away from the fire toward the darker edge of the clearing, where I thought I could enjoy a bit more anonymity until Emily showed up. After the heat I had felt on my skin, closer to the fire, here I was a little cold. There wasn't much I could do until Emily showed up, so I stood there, peering into the scene, trying to find a familiar face. I was doing that when words simply popped up in my head.

Turn around, they said. It was an order, but not a threatening one—that's the best way I can describe it. It threw me off balance for a moment, and the novel experience was a bit scary, but then I pulled myself together and turned around. I gazed into the dark and saw nothing.

I knew it! The voice in my head said again, and this time it sounded triumphant.

I had to do something to respond to this situation. Someone had made mind contact with me! I had always thought that to accomplish bidirectional mind conversations, you had to have a real, personal connection with the other person, like I briefly had with Bill. Even then, it had taken an effort to lower all the barriers to allow us to "speak" telepathically. But if he could send me a message without my help—and it was a "he," the voice had a clear masculine consistency—then I had to be able to do the same. Sending thought messages is not quite the same as reading minds, and I had never done that point-blank before. I didn't know if I was doing it right or transmitting it at all, but I instinctively felt how I should do it. *Who are you?* I formed the thought in my mind and "pushed" it out with all my mental strength.

Take a few steps ahead, and you'll see me, the voice in my head said again. I debated whether to do as instructed, but only briefly. Maybe I was walking into a trap, but I had proven to myself in the past that I can take care of myself. Whatever it took, I had to find out who was connecting with me. It was simply not something I could avoid or postpone. I took a step toward the darker side of the woods, then another, and then a third. I saw a shape in the distance waving at me. I got closer, and then I stopped.

"Jamie!" I exclaimed.

CHAPTER 7

Now you might ask me how stupid I must be to follow someone I don't know well into a dark, secluded place. But you can't judge without knowing what a telepathic connection means. I didn't know it either before meeting Jamie. The only telepathic connection I had had before was with Bill. But here's the thing—although a telepath can stop another from reading his thoughts, he cannot hide his real emotions. Those come across as "feeling images," or, as I like to call them, "telemoticons," now that I have much more experience with them than I had then in those woods. They don't have a defined shape or color you can draw or explain, but they are a subtext that gives meaning to the words. You cannot tell somebody, "I like you," if you dislike him; the telemoticon accompanying those words immediately tells him you're lying.

So now you'll understand why I trusted Jamie. In my mind, his words said *Don't worry, you're safe with me*, and the telemoticon that came with the words added exclamation marks to that statement.

That doesn't mean that I was happy when he guided me into a cold, creepy crypt in the cemetery.

"Why do we need to go in there?" I asked. We had switched automatically to regular speech.

"There is much that you need to know and other people that you should meet, and it's not safe to do that out in the open. Also, the stone above us is thick; that makes reading us or eavesdropping on a telepathic conversation from the outside difficult, if not impossible. That is why we meet here."

"'We' being who?"

"Patience. In a moment," he said.

We had reached a grated door with a heavy, rusty lock; Jamie took a key from his pocket and opened it. A short corridor took us to a small chamber. We had been using our cell phones to light our way in the dark hall. Now Jamie flipped a switch, and two weak light bulbs illuminated the room enough for me to see its details. A marble table was all it contained, but two niches held what appeared to be coffins.

"Don't worry, they're empty," he said, as if reading my mind—well, I guess I wasn't paying attention, and he was reading it.

"That's the least of my worries," I said. "Please explain all this."

"Come here, sit," said Jamie. The marble table was low, and he had seated himself on it. I went and sat by his side. I gazed at him, waiting for him to go on. He cleared his throat and hesitated for a moment. "This must look weird to you," he said at last.

"Weird doesn't begin to define it. It's starting to look like a *Raiders of the Lost Ark* movie or something. All this secrecy and crypts. How did you know that I was a telepath? I knew that there must be someone else with telepathic powers out there—I had already met one, briefly; he's dead now—but it's amazing that you got on to me so quickly."

"Not so strange. After all, you aren't the first."

"The first what?"

"The first government agent they sent to kill us."

I don't know if you ever found yourself trapped in a spooky underground crypt with someone who accuses you of wanting to kill him. Probably not, and I can tell you that the thoughts that would pass through your mind if you were would not be happy ones. Mine came and grew more and more unpleasant when I heard the grated door squeak, meaning that others were coming. A few seconds later, Tracy and Thomas walked in.

Tracy had introduced Thomas briefly to me at the poolside during Nate's party, and I had thought him a hundred percent uninteresting. He was a beefy guy who shook my hand limply without looking me in the eyes. *God,* I had thought then, *who shakes a girl's hand at a party? Who is this guy, a traveling sales-man?* But then Tracy had dragged me away to meet more people, and I had forgotten all about him. I do that when people don't interest me; I delete them from my memory.

"You got her here. Good for you, Jamie," Thomas said. "What are we going to do with her? We can't let her go," he added ominously.

"Nothing, she's okay," said Jamie.

"Told you so," Tracy interjected.

"Nonsense!" said Thomas, and then he turned to me. "Do you deny that you are a government agent?" he asked.

As a general rule, I'm not one to remain speechless when someone attacks me. You don't want to get in my line of fire when I'm pissed off, but this time I had to be careful what I said because I had no idea what this was all about.

"Listen, about that nonsense of coming here to kill you—I've come to kill no one, okay? I don't know what you're talking about."

"She's telling the truth," Jamie said. Those telemoticons again, I guess.

"All right. So why are you here?" Thomas insisted.

I knew I had no choice but to come clean, and I did. I told them everything—the institute, the information leak, my mission. It went against my basic training and professional conscience, but lying to them wasn't an option because they would have got on to me in a second. All I could do was give as few details as possible.

"They're using you as bait," Tracy murmured.

"What do you mean?"

"Explain, Jamie. This will take time."

"You need to know that we are not unique," Jamie said. "There are many like us who live in hiding. I'm surprised that we seem to be the only ones in Emendale, but perhaps others hide as we do. Five years ago, when I lived in a big city, a telepath decided to stop hiding. He placed ads in newspapers, calling to other telepaths to join him. He raked up a few followers, and they started to meet and compare their abilities. You will learn that we are not all the same. Some of us have certain capabilities that others don't have."

"I never heard about this. Working in my field, I would have expected the government to know about it and tell me."

'Oh, the government knows all right. They knew about those meetings and the people who participated, and they went after them. Two years ago, they met up in the mountains at a cabin for a weekend retreat and telepathic training. The official story was that a fire erupted in the cabin at night, killing everybody. In reality, the government raided the cabin and murdered everyone."

"How awful! But how can you know? Can't it be that there really was a fire?"

Jamie swallowed twice before responding. The emotion clearly showed on his face as he recalled the incident.

"My girlfriend, Anne, was at the retreat. Our father refused to let me and Tracy go, and I got like crazy mad at him. He's not a telepath, but he has intuitions, and when he gets worried about something, there is no hope to change his mind. I had looked forward to this weekend with Anne and maybe a little also to doing some cool telepathic stuff there. He couldn't explain it to himself, but he said that he had a bad feeling about it. When the government assassins came, I was talking to Anne, telepathically, of course. I saw everything through her eyes. That's how I know it wasn't a fire."

"Poor Jamie!" I said. I felt his pain, and it almost choked me. My hand went instinctively to squeeze his arm for comfort. He relaxed a little and went on.

"That very night, we left town. My father is rich and had understood early on that we might end up being in grave danger someday. He had prepared escape options for a contingency like that, so we changed names and moved to this place, hiding in plain sight as it is because there is government research done here, and it's a small community but one where people keep to themselves. We hoped that Emandale was a remote and sleepy enough place to keep us safe. But as it turns out, it isn't."

"And what about you, Thomas?"

"I wasn't a part of that group, but Jamie and I have been friends since the cradle, so he insisted I come with them when they left. I live with my mother, and she was scared enough to jump at the opportunity."

"I don't understand," I said. "None of this makes sense. The governmental agency where I work is dying to find more people like me to work with them. Only a couple of months ago, they sent me to find a telepath that they thought lived nearby. They have a machine that can tell you if there is a telepathic activity, but not exactly where; it isn't very sophisticated. They wanted to recruit him, but unfortunately, there was a hit-and-run accident, and he died."

"They used you to locate him, and then he died?" Tracy asked.

Her tone spoke volumes, and suddenly, the enormity of the thing dawned on me.

"Oh, my God!" I whispered.

"My God is right," said Thomas acidly. "That's their plan for us too. You expose us, and then some freakish accident happens to us."

If they were right, it had to mean that Mary was in on it too ... and Liv? Liv wouldn't, or would she?

"They sent me here with two field operatives who play my father and mother, but they can't be in on it too because I would know. They can't know if I am reading them and finding out what they are up to. So maybe you're wrong."

I know that I was clutching at straws, but the alternative was too scary to think of. Could that be why Liv convinced me to use telepathy only if I must? To keep Mom and Dad safe from my reading them? I couldn't believe it.

"They don't need to know anything until they get the order," said Jamie. "If tomorrow they receive an order to terminate Tracy —sorry, Sis, just an example—or you, they'll do it without asking questions."

I didn't think Bob would kill me if he got the order or betray me in any way. He had made it clear that he was personally invested in protecting me. For a moment, I wondered how he would deal with the conflict if it ever arose, but then I chased that thought away.

"So, what do we do?" For the first time in a long time, I was confused and had no action plan.

"We buy time," said Jamie. "You go back to your 'parents' as if nothing happened and make them believe it's business as usual."

"But what good is it going to do? They will keep looking for you, with or without my help."

"We have a plan. It's not only us in this."

"You're talking too much, Jamie," Thomas interrupted. "We can't trust her that far. Even if we are resigned to putting our lives in danger, we can't place everybody else in jeopardy. Government operatives have techniques to hide information and thoughts in their minds, too deep for you to find simply by reading them. You know that. Even if I agree that, on the face of it, Alex here is okay, that doesn't mean that I'm right."

"I can check her out," said Tracy. "Come here," she ordered me.

"How can you do that?" I asked.

"We told you that everybody has different abilities. I am a TAR telepath. I knew only another one like me, but he was killed in that mountain cabin, so that makes me kind of unique," she said with a sad smile. "I have a combined touch-and-read ability. If I read you while we are touching, I can reach the deepest level of your mind. There is nothing you can hide from me, no matter how good the control of your mind is. Once I'm through with it, I'll know you as well as you know yourself. Better, probably, because we all hide things from ourselves. Does that scare you, or are you ready to go through with it?"

I hesitated only for a moment. Like everybody else, I have things that I don't want to be exposed for the whole world to see. Some things are too intimate to tell anybody, but I didn't have anything to hide from them regarding my work with the government.

"I'm not scared. I don't scare easily," I said, "and I'm ready to be checked by you on one condition."

"What?"

"You'll see facets of me that I like to keep to myself. I want your word that you won't tell anybody what you have seen."

"You have my word. All these boys will hear from me is that you can or cannot be trusted with what we have to tell you."

"Careful, Sis. You need to do this right. The stakes are too high to allow for mistakes."

"I'll be thorough, don't worry. You know I am."

She beckoned to me, and I jumped down from the table and

stood before her. She took my hands and guided me to hold her waist like in a dancing posture, and then she placed her hands on my shoulders and pulled me closer. She ran her lips lightly over my cheek and neck, sending a shiver along my spine.

"I need to feel you closer," she whispered.

"I ... don't mind," I whispered back. I honestly didn't.

She held me like that for a long minute. I felt her breath on my face and an almost imperceptible vibration coming from her body. Her eyes were closed, but she didn't need to see me. She was in my head, and the experience was something I had never felt before, a sensation that we were becoming one, melding together. I let go of all the automatic barriers that my brain puts up when someone is trying to read me, and it felt as if I was completely bare and helpless. That's when she kissed my mouth—a sensuous kiss that acted like the final piece of a puzzle locking together the finished shape. I responded to her kiss, which I did uncharacteristically timidly, and it was as if the very essence of my being was passed on to her through it. I felt like a vortex was drawing us in together, sucked into a kaleidoscopic view of lights and skies. For a moment, I lost touch with myself and felt suspended in a void. Then she stopped, gently pushed me away, opened her eyes, and turned to the boys.

"We can trust her fully. She's all she said she is, and a lot more that I won't tell you guys," she added, giving me a conspiratorial glance. "Her real name is Tessa. I like it better than Alex."

"Welcome to our little group of fugitives, Tessa," Jamie said and smiled.

I was still dazzled by the feelings that the intimate mind contact with Tracy had given me. I realized that it would take me a little while to be my old, practical self again, but I had to make an effort. I managed to smile back and nod to acknowledge the welcome.

"So, what now?"

"Now you'll learn how big this whole picture is. It's time for you to meet Daddy."

CHAPTER 8

Jamie's and Tracy's father was a handsome, blue-eyed man of about forty-five, tall, elegant, with black hair and manicured hands. His name was Nolan, or at least that was the name he was going under at the time. He was not at all who I expected the father of two red-headed twins to be. As it turned out, they had taken their red hair from their mother, along with their telepathic ability. She had passed away when they were little, and Nolan had raised them all by himself. He was a businessman, and his work kept him free to come and go as he pleased without coming under the scrutiny of the local gossip. He maintained a decorous life, as befitting a widower, discouraging people from getting too close, and for a good reason, as I later learned.

"Dad, meet Alex," Tracy said as we walked into their elegant but not showy home, a nice contrast to Nate's. Thomas had somehow vanished along the way, which was all right with me. I felt uncomfortable with him around because he still couldn't hide his hostility to me.

"Ha, yes, Alex ... I have heard much about you. Did you have a good time at the bonfire? Come, sit down," he said, and then he pointed two fingers at his temple in an explicit request, meaning, "Read me!"

I obliged.

Are you reading me? he thought, and when I nodded, he continued. *We never speak about these things. We never know who's listening. For all I know, the house may be bugged. The kids wanted me to tell you what we think you should know, and I will, but you'll have to read me for it.*

"Do you like music?" he asked out loud, puzzling me.

"Sure," I said, "why are you asking?"

"I was about to listen to a Chopin piano concert that I'm sure you'll like."

"I'm not really into old people's music," I said and immediately regretted it when Jamie's thoughts danced before my eyes.

Dad can't explain to you and talk simultaneously, he intervened. *When we need to do that in the house, we listen to music, so if anybody's eavesdropping on us, he won't find it strange that we don't speak.*

"... but I'm always open to new experiences, and I'll be happy to try this one out. Chopin, you say? I heard he is kind of okay."

Nolan turned the music on, and we sat down "to listen." Reporting our conversation in full would be tedious, so I'll give you the gist. I read him and asked questions, mostly by lifting eyebrows or making smart comments about the concert. It turns out that telepaths' persecution is nothing new; it has been going on for decades. Nolan had learned about it after meeting and falling in love with his wife. The twins' mother was active in TAG —the Telepath Action Group—a movement founded by a mystical figure known as Mark. Nobody knew who Mark was, only that he had been working with a government agency when he discovered the plot to kill each and every telepath. It seems that the government considered us more dangerous than a lethal virus, so we had to be exterminated.

Mark established fifteen separate cells, each with a few

telepaths, like the one we had here, designated "cell 13." From his hiding place, he coordinated the activity of all cells. They mainly concentrated on doing what it took to stay alive and bring in telepaths from other places. The endgame was to allow these small communities to grow and reach a critical mass that might make it safe to go public. Exposing the telepathic community to the world might stop the genocide, which so far had been perpetrated in silence.

There are many other telepaths out there who are hiding. We need to find them and bring them in.

Wow!

And what was I to do with all this information? I asked, pointing a finger at myself and making a clueless face. Nolan's answer was, *I discussed it with the kids. They'll fill you in, but not now.*

At last, Chopin had given up with a few final notes, so it was time for me to go and try to make some sense out of all this.

"The concert was amazing, Mr. Walsh," I said, "thank you. I guess it's time for me to go home."

"Call me Nolan, please. No need to be formal with my children's friends."

"Thank you, Nolan. I hope that you'll invite me to listen to some more music in the future. I liked this one."

And I had honestly liked it—at least the bits I had managed to hear during my "conversation" with Nolan. Funny, right?

"I'll walk you home," Jamie said.

"You don't need to—" I started to say, but he cut me short.

"I insist," he said, and to my mind, he added, *We need to talk.*

"Well, thank you. It's nice of you. What about you, Tracy?" I asked.

"I'll stay," she said.

I nodded and was about to go when Tracy pushed a thought into my head. *He really likes you*, it said. She smiled what I guess she thought was a meaningful smile, and then she left.

I only wished that she had specified who "he" was. Just so I would be sure.

"Good night, Nolan, and thanks again for the music," I said.

"Good night."

"Night, Dad," said Jamie, and we walked out.

Jamie and I walked silently, each with our own thoughts, until we reached a bus stop on the way to where my happy little fake family lived.

"Let's sit here for a while, okay?" he said.

"You gave me quite a bit to chew on, you know?" I said after we sat down. We were alone in the empty street, but I still found myself whispering.

"Yes, and I'm sorry, but there is more. When you're ready."

"Look, I like being a telepath, but do we need all that cloak-and-dagger stuff? All those methods of covert communication are giving me a headache. I prefer that we speak here, out in the open, where nobody is listening. Okay with you?"

"I prefer that too, but I needed you and Dad to get acquainted. He makes all the decisions, and he's the one who's keeping us alive … at least so far, so he had to see you, and you had to hear him tell the story."

"I understand. I just need a little time to process all that information."

"Let's hope that we have time," Jamie said.

"What do you mean?"

"Things are precipitating. Dad thinks that if the government sent a telepath—you—over here, that means an operation is brewing."

"What a mess!"

"Yes, isn't it? But I don't want to worry you more than I already have tonight. We can talk about it tomorrow morning. I'll pick you up at nine for mushroom hunting in the forest."

"I know nothing about mushrooms," I protested.

"Neither do I. Be ready with a nice basket. Make some sandwiches; it may be a long morning. I'll bring the beer."

I realized with a tingle along my spine that I was looking forward to it. Not to the mushroom nonsense, to spending the morning with Jamie in the woods. I never blush (or so I say), but I felt a rush of blood to my cheek and jumped up.

"It's getting fuckin' cold. Take me home," I ordered and started walking.

The damn telemoticons!

CHAPTER 9

Mom put the plate of eggs before me and stood there for a few seconds, gazing down at me. That's when I knew that she was wondering about something. That's also when I realized I had to start reading Mom and Dad often to keep myself safe.

She's a bit strange this morning. I wonder what happened at the bonfire, she thought. Good, that was a line of thought I could work with.

"You know, Mom," I said out loud, "I met a boy yesterday, and I think he can be useful to get me launched into school society. We are going mushroom picking today."

As I said that, I thought of Jamie, and I think I even managed to blush a little.

"You remember that tomorrow is the first day of school, right? I hope that getting involved with this boy is not going to harm your studies," said Dad.

Translation: You can't lose focus. You are on a mission.

"Don't worry. To succeed in my studies, I must get to know people and have a social life," I said, which sounded quite incongruous, but I knew they understood what I meant. "This boy is very popular and will introduce me to a lot of people. I know what I'm doing."

She's lying. She likes this boy, I can tell, was Mom's thought.

Well played! I congratulated myself.

"As long as you keep that in mind and remember that your studies are the most important thing ...," said Dad.

I read him too, but his thoughts had already turned to the newspaper he had spread on the breakfast table, so I knew he wasn't worried at all.

Before I left, I gave him back the watch he had made me wear the night of the bonfire.

"It's too ugly for words. Don't make me wear it again. I was in no danger," I said.

He merely nodded and took it.

The surprise was when Jamie showed up on a scooter. He handed a pink scooter helmet to me, and I raised an eyebrow.

"It's Tracy's," he hastened to say.

"Don't you have a proper car?" I teased him.

"I do, but the scooter is better for today. It can take us deep into the woods where a car cannot pass."

"Up on your steed, then," I said and jumped on.

Jamie was a careful driver, and most of the time, the ride was smooth, at least until we got off-road, and then it became a bit bumpy. I had to hold onto him, and because the seat was short, I kept a tight grip on him. It was kind of pleasant when I felt his warmth, except when occasionally our helmets knocked into each other. Eventually, the path that we had been following took us to the bottom of a steep hill. Jamie stopped the scooter and killed the engine.

"Time to walk," he said, taking off his helmet.

"Where to?"

"To the top of this hill. It's only a ten-minute walk and a beautiful one. You'll like it. I'll carry the basket."

I handed him the basket with the sandwiches I had made, and he added two beers to it. We started walking uphill through thick woods. The air was cool, and the scent of pine resin and other wild growth was strong. At one point, I slipped on the wet forest floor and almost fell, but Jamie got hold of my hand and helped me to keep my balance. After that, he didn't let go of my hand, and I let him walk with me hand in hand until we reached the top.

The view from the top of the hill was spectacular. You could see the town on one side and wild nature far away on the other. The day was clear, so we had a view reaching miles away. Jamie spread the blanket he had carried on his shoulder tied with a string, and we sat down.

"Breathtaking," I said. I felt I had to say something.

"This is my favorite place. I like to come here, alone, and think. You are the first person I ever brought here."

"What an honor!" I joked.

Jamie's face turned serious, and his gaze focused far away.

"Sometimes I think that we can't win. I don't know what I would do if it weren't for my father and Tracy. You don't know what it is like, knowing that people are after you to kill you, people around you have been killed, and you can't do anything about it. Here is where I go when I feel like that. It's kind of a special place for me."

"Listen, Jamie," I said softly, "I know exactly how you feel. I've had people plotting to kill me and acting on their plans, and I've had people dying as a result." I didn't tell him that I had had to kill at least two of them. Somehow, I thought it wouldn't go down well with him. "But I never thought I was helpless, and neither should you. You're fighting back, and that makes you powerful. And I appreciate it that you've brought me here, to this place that is so special to you, because—"

Here I had to stop speaking, not because I had run out of things to say, but because Jamie was kissing me so hard that all I could do was breathe through my nose.

I analyzed my feelings. I can do it in a detached way, even in the middle of intensive action. I've done that when in mortal danger, and doing it now was not hard. Except that I had to find out what that thumping sound was. It couldn't be my heart, could it?

It was.

"One moment," I said breathlessly, once Jamie paused, "I need to check something."

Jamie breathed heavily, his eyes fixed on me, and he wasn't speaking.

"Let me read you," I said after encountering an unsurmountable barrier in his mind. "Close your eyes," I ordered as soon as he lifted the barrier.

Now it was my turn to kiss him. I read and kissed, kissed and read until I was satisfied that I knew all I needed to know.

"You check out," I said, "you need to kiss me some more."

The next few minutes didn't involve telepathy, merely feeling one another and kissing like two teenagers. It gave me the illusion of being normal for a little while, and that was worth so much that I can't explain. After the first wave of intense emotion passed, I propped myself on one elbow. I kept massaging his chest lightly with my free hand to keep the contact going.

"There's something that I learned from Tracy," I said. "I'm not a TAR telepath, but reading and kissing simultaneously somehow gives me a deeper insight."

"And did you like what you saw?"

"Boy, if the way I kissed you right now hasn't given you the answer to that, you're a lost cause."

"It kind of did, I guess. You dug deep inside my head, you know? It's still tingling because of it."

"I had to. Interesting stuff you have in there."

"So, now what?"

"Now I'm hungry. Get the sandwiches and open those beers, will you?"

We ate in silence. Somehow, we didn't need to speak right then. I had a lot to process after seeing some deep layers of Jamie's mind, and some of it bothered me. At last, I had to say something.

"I like you," I said, "a lot. But so you know, I don't do love."

"What does that even mean, 'you don't do love'? And when did I say that I was in love with you?"

"You didn't say it because you haven't fallen in love with me, yet. But you're dangerously close to it, and I don't want you to get hurt. I don't do love because I don't want people I love to get hurt."

"You know you're not making any sense at all, right?"

"Yes, it's hard to explain with words. Read me."

I opened my mind a little, enough for him to understand how I felt and what I meant. I sensed him reading me and saw the emotions reflected on his face. When he was through reading, I gave him a quick kiss.

"You see now?" I asked.

"Girls are crazy," he said, "but I guess I understand a little."

"Good."

"So we'll see where this is going without making a big deal of it, right?"

I nodded. I had seen Jamie's inner vulnerability, and I knew I couldn't let him down, or it might break him. Losing Anne the way he had, before his eyes, had left a permanent wound in his soul. I wasn't going to be the one to push him over the edge.

"Let's talk shop, then," I said to change the subject. "What do you think we should do?"

"I spoke with my father and the others. We think that the most urgent thing is to find out if there is anybody else, someone in school, who is working with the government. We call him or her 'Tray,' by the way, code name for 'traitor.'"

"I can work on that, but wait—if he is one of the people in high school, you would have gotten on to this Tray already, right? You've known everybody for two years now. Why would I be any better at this than you are?"

"Because you are a government agent, so you can advertise yourself as such to Tray if he exists at all. It's only speculation. But if the government has an agent on-site, with you, he doesn't need to hide; you're on the same side."

"Hmm, I'm not sure it's a good idea or that it will be that easy, but I can try. You'll need a Plan B, though, for if I fail."

"We don't have a Plan B, except running away again to some other place, but we don't want to spend our lives running and hiding," said Jaime, speaking moodily. He got up and started to collect the remains of our picnic. "Time to go back," he said.

He rolled up the blanket, tied it with its string, and gazed at me inquisitively, seeing that I wasn't moving. I took two steps toward him. His hands were full, so I put mine on his shoulders and kissed him long and softly.

"One for the road," I said when I took a step back from him. His smile was so broad that I realized that keeping a distance from him would be a full-time job.

That evening as I lay in bed, I realized I hadn't thought about Liv for two full days. Was I missing her? Did I doubt her? I realized that I was both. I closed my eyes and brought her face before my mind's eye. A moment later, I was in her head. It didn't feel right, although I had been there many times before. It didn't because it had always been with her blessing until now, and she had always known when I was doing it, but now I was spying on her. She was watching TV, a soap opera, and an almost empty bottle of wine and a solitary glass were on her side table. Her mind was confused, and I realized that she was drunk. She had never been a heavy drinker, which wasn't in her character.

Distance does have an effect when reading somebody's mind. When I was with Liv, touching and feeling her close, I always reached deep levels of her soul, pretty much like it had happened with Jamie on that hill. But when I read someone from a distance, the reading is much more superficial without any physical contact. What I can see is what is on the mind of the person I read at the time of reading.

I probed Liv's mind gently, trying to see if any troubling thoughts were going through it, but there was little to see there. She was following the soap opera in a fuzzy sort of way. She allowed the images and the sounds to go through her brain without paying too much attention. I felt like an invader, probing her mind, which was vulnerable right then. I had to let her know that I was there; I couldn't help myself. I took control of her left hand and lifted it to her cheek, then caressed it gently and let go of her. She would know that I was there, and I hoped she would speak to me. Instead, she took her hand up to her cheek again and scratched it to cancel the soft sensation of my caress.

I felt as if she had hit me. In a flash, I disconnected from Liv's mind and found myself back in the darkness of my temporary room. I curled up in bed, feeling a lump growing in my throat. Liv was rejecting me, as she had done when I had phoned her. There had to be a reason for it, which I couldn't understand, but I felt betrayed regardless. I curled up a bit more, ignoring a tear slowly flowing down my cheek, and I breathed myself deeply to sleep.

CHAPTER 10

Monday, first day in school. I was excited like a little girl and had to remind myself that this wasn't for real. This wasn't my real world, merely a fake life created to ferret people out. Still, I lingered while picking out my clothes and putting on some makeup. I don't put on makeup unless it's for a party or a date, but the first day in school felt a little like a party. I wondered what Mary would have said if she could have read my thoughts. She wasn't a prude, far from it, but after they had made her head of the Extra-Sensory Unit, she insisted that I keep a more business-like dress code. *Screw Mary,* I thought, *I can have a little fun while I'm doing her dirty job, right? After all, she's government, and the government wants to exterminate the likes of me, so that means that Mary wants to eliminate me. So it means that Liv ... I need to stop thinking these things!* I shook my head to chase those thoughts away. I knew they weren't going to do me any good. Instead, I pasted a forced smile on my lips and walked down the stairs.

"Ready to go?" Mom asked.

"As ready as I will ever be," I said. "I'll grab a coffee and something to eat, and then you can drive me to school."

I read her for a little while, but her thoughts dwelled on pancakes, eggs, and coffee, all pretty innocent, so I stopped. She put a plate with twice the amount of food I could eat in a day before me.

"You need to grow, honey," she said.

I had started to hate her for being so good at playing the fake mommy, and, for some reason, this forced show of sweetness got on my nerves.

I got out of the car and stood on the lawn, taking in the impressive school building.

"Hi, Alex! Are you lost?" a voice called behind me, and I turned to see Emily.

"Hi," I said. "I was savoring my last minutes of freedom from school, but you're right; I have no clue where to go right now."

"Our first class today is biology. It starts in five minutes, so we'd better get moving."

I followed her into the school and through a corridor into a class. That school building was ancient, and its halls were winding. Without Emily, I would have gotten lost and been late for my first lesson. As I walked into the class, Nate got up and beckoned me.

"Alex, here!" he cried. "I've saved you a place next to me."

"Thank you," I said, "but I'm here with Emily."

I sat beside her, and she made a face at Nate, who made one back and sat down alone without another word. Eventually, a freckled girl came in and sat beside him without waiting for an invitation.

The lesson was as boring as it gets. A fat teacher with thin hair and a sickly-white complexion gave us a preview of what we would do that semester, and it all went over my head. The rest of the day wasn't much different, except that the monotonous repetition applied to history, mathematics, and chemistry. Between two lessons, I went outside—I needed fresh air. Tracy walked up to me when there was nobody around.

"Can you come to my house tonight, say at seven?" she asked.

"Sure, what's up?"

"We have more things to talk about."

"I'll be there," I said.

"Good," said Tracy and walked away.

I wondered if she was being distant for real or if that was an act for the benefit of whoever was watching us to avoid being seen as too close. No use fretting about it, though. I would know that evening.

I found an old bike in the toolshed of the house. Its tires were flat, but it had a pump attached to it, and I managed to return it to working condition. It was a boy's bike with a straight top tube, but it would have to do. Dad didn't like the idea.

"That thing is dangerous; I can drive you wherever you want," he protested.

"That's how you want people here to perceive me, like I'm attached to my parents' apron strings all the time? No thanks. I can ride a bike; I've done it since I was five years old."

"All right, but be careful. I worry about you; I really do. I'm afraid you may be overconfident sometimes, which could be dangerous."

"Yes, Daddy," I said, making a mocking curtsy.

Cheeky girl, she thinks she knows best, he thought while I read him, and then he added something that worried me—*As soon as I hear back from them, we'll see about it.*

Hear back from them? Who were they? If he was having conversations I was unaware of with Headquarters, it might mean trouble. I tried to read him some more, but his thoughts had turned to the gardening he was doing outside. You had to hand it to him—he was thorough at building his fake image, or maybe he was simply enjoying the quiet, small-town life and the gardening. I would have to find a time to read him when he wasn't thinking intensively about something specific; then, I might learn who he was waiting to hear back from and what about.

I pushed that worry aside and jumped on the bike. It had been years since I had ridden a bicycle, and I had missed pedaling and feeling the wind on my face. The surroundings were pleasant, the air cool, and all I had to do was keep my mouth shut to avoid swallowing too many mosquitos. I enjoyed the ride. I propped the bike against a large vase before Tracy's house and pushed the bell. In a few seconds, Tracy opened the door.

"Hi, you're punctual. Do you want to go for a walk?" she asked.

I hesitated for a second, and then a thought popped up in my head—*That wasn't a question. We need to go.*

"Sure, a walk. Yes, I like to walk."

Tracy closed the door behind her, and we walked in silence until we reached an open stretch of the road.

"What is this all about?" I asked.

"We need to go to the crypt. Everybody's waiting for us there. We always go separately and in different ways, but I wanted to talk to you, so I asked you to come to my house and not there directly."

"Good, because I don't know what got into you. You talk in telegraphic bursts like you're mad at me."

"I'm not mad at you, but I'm worried. About Jamie."

"Ah, so that's it ..."

"Yes, that's it. I don't know if you understand, but he's very fragile."

"He doesn't look fragile to me at all."

"Mentally, I mean."

"I know about Anne and what it has done to him. He let me read him."

Tracy stopped, turned to me, and grabbed my arm.

"So you know that he hurts and can't bear much more pain. Look, I like you very much, but he's falling for you, and if you let that happen and then you hurt him ..."

Her voice broke, and she stopped in mid-sentence. It was my time to take hold of her. I pulled her close and hugged her.

"Read me now, and you'll know that I'll never hurt him. I understand what you're saying, and I won't let that happen."

"I believe you. Thank you," she said, and I released the hug.

There was a tear running down her cheek, and I knew what it was for—it was for what she and I could have had if it wouldn't hurt her brother. Reading in an emotional state runs both ways. I wiped the tear with my finger and caressed her cheek.

"We are going to be good friends, you and me," I said.

"Yes."

"You know Jamie far better than I do, and there is no doubt that he is sensitive, but don't make him a pussy. He's strong and has character. He will get over his bad experience; it only takes time."

"He will," she said and started walking again.

"Each time I go into that crypt, it feels like I'm never coming out again," said Tracy.

"Yeah, it's creepy, but let's make sure there's nobody around. Imagine if some maniac saw us going in there and came after us," I said and laughed.

It was a nervous laugh, though. I'm courageous, but that place creeped me out.

"Thank you, now you're scaring the shit out of me," Tracy complained.

We stopped at the entrance to the corridor leading to the crypt, scanning the surroundings. There was nobody around except us, so we walked in. We reached the grated door, and the voices that came from inside the crypt reassured us. I wouldn't have liked to go in and find the place empty. A few more steps got us into the crypt itself. Jamie was sitting on the low table like the first night we had met there, and Thomas was drawing circles in the dust with his shoe. When they saw us, Jamie jumped down and smiled.

"It was time you got here," Thomas said, speaking morosely.

"We walked," Tracy said, shrugging.

"Well, now that you're here, we need to start," said Jamie, speaking conciliatorily. "I'll go first."

"Why don't you explain the purpose of this meeting first," I said.

"You're right. As you know by now, not all telepaths are the same. Each of us has different abilities, and now that you are one of us, we need to know exactly what yours are. Of course, you also need to know what we can do so that we can do things together in the best way."

"That makes sense."

"I am a pusher and a hooker," said Jamie, smiling broadly.

"That sounds interesting," I said, smiling back. "I hope it's a bit less literal than it sounds."

"Right. I am a pusher because I can push thoughts into your head. You've experienced it yourself. I can do that with regular people too, I think. I've tried it with my father, and it works with him, but I haven't tried it with anybody else, and it may be that it only works because we are close; I don't know. I can't try it with anybody else."

"Okay, that takes care of the pusher," I said, "but I really want to hear about the hooker."

"That's a bit more tricky. I can push a thought into your head that allows me to hook to your mind and see through your eyes if you hold on to it. It doesn't come easily, and I need to practice with you, but after a while, it becomes natural." Jamie was silent for a moment, his gaze suddenly went far away, and I knew what memory this had brought up for him. "It's what we were doing when ..." he started to say.

"It's like when two computers do a handshake," Thomas hastened to say, and I understood that he wanted to stop Jamie's train of thought.

"Please don't talk nerdish to me; I don't know how you can waste your time with those computer thingies," Tracy added, helping too.

"Anyway, that's it," said Jamie, looking at us as if he was seeing us again. "That's what I can do. Your turn, Tommy."

"I am a pretty boring kind of telepath," said Thomas with a sigh. "All I can do is read people's thoughts as long as they are in the room with me and I can see them. Nothing flashy, really. No pushing or other cool stuff, I'm afraid."

On the way there, I had asked Tracy about Thomas.

"What's the deal with Thomas?" I had asked.

"He's a friend of Jamie from kindergarten, you know. I think he's dumb, but Jamie loves him. He refused to leave home without him, so we had to talk to his mother, Sandie, and explain the situation to her. Dad scared the hell out of her so she would agree to up and come with us. She was a nurse, the same as she does here, and it took some convincing to get her on board. Since then, we have been stuck with Thomas. I tolerate him for Jamie's sake, but I can't bring myself to be nice to him."

That made a lot of sense from what I had seen and from Thomas' lackluster exposition.

Then it was Tracy's turn. I knew she was interesting, but I wasn't prepared for what she showed us.

"I know that you have this touch-and-read ability to dig deep into people's souls—I've experienced it myself, but what else can you do?" I asked.

"I can chat telepathically; you know that too. And I can get weird."

"What do you mean 'weird'?"

"I'll show you."

Tracy stood there in silence, gazing at me. As I watched her, she suddenly turned into a marble cherub, like those disposed around the crypt. It was an unexpected, creepy, and awe-inspiring experience. It lasted for a minute, and then she was Tracy again.

"Holy cow!" I said, and I meant it. "How did you do that?"

Tracy gave a little laugh, obviously pleased with herself and with my surprise. I guess that my jaw had dropped.

"I can send out an image of myself that makes you see me like what I want. If I pick an image close to the background, as I did now, I can fully disappear for you. It would have been harder if I wanted to become a blue-and-red garden gnome."

"That's positively awesome, Tracy. I've never seen anything like that. Do you target one person or everybody around you?"

"We all saw Sis become a cherub," said Jamie. "She used to annoy me when we were kids and make me believe I was seeing Batman, Superman, or Santa Claus. I'd beat her up every time she played that trick on me."

"That's a neat mind trick if I've ever seen one," I said. "And it may come in very useful sometime."

"Well, now it's your turn," said Jamie.

"Okay, all right. Let me see where to start. I can read you and chat, pretty much like Tracy. If I know you—even only from a picture—I can find you and get into your head from a distance, even if you're thousands of miles away. So I can read any normal person, wherever he is. I assume that it will work with bidirectional chatting too, but I haven't had an opportunity to try it. Anyway, I can see no reason why it won't work."

"That's amazing! That's powerful! You're a much stronger telepath than we are or that I've ever heard of," said Thomas, suddenly arising to enthusiasm.

"Wow! I mean, wow!" Jamie added.

"Ehm ... there is something else."

"What?" Jamie and Thomas asked in unison.

"I need to show it to you. I need a volunteer for that."

"Look, now you're starting to spook me," said Jamie.

"I'll volunteer," said Thomas.

"All right. Please don't worry," I reassured him, "nothing bad will happen, but it may feel a bit unusual."

"Just get on with it, okay?"

I nodded and closed my eyes. A second later or less, I was in Thomas' brain, so I reopened my eyes and gazed at him. I made him go slowly down on his knees, keeping a frozen face, and then I spoke through his mouth.

"This is me, Tessa, speaking to you with Thomas's voice. I have taken possession of his body, as you can see. I will release my hold on him in a second."

Slowly, to avoid jerky movements, I released my hold on Thomas. He jumped up to his feet, looking positively scared. I couldn't blame him; I knew how terrifying being possessed could be when you didn't expect it.

"You're the devil!" Thomas spurted out.

"You're the Queen Bee!" Jamie said, speaking with awe.

"You're something," Tracy said simply.

"So, you can do that to anybody? And what happens when you're inside their head?" Jamie asked.

"When I'm inside a person's head, whether I am taking possession of his body or not, I feel all the sensations he feels—touch, smell, taste, everything. And yes, I can do it to anybody."

"Incredible, amazing," said Jamie. "Mark must be told."

"Reaching Mark is not that easy. We need to talk to Dad," said Tracy.

Jamie pursed his lips as if in deep thought, and then he turned to me, speaking quietly and softly.

"I knew you were something special," he said, "I knew that instinctively, but I didn't know how much."

Thomas said nothing. He had gone back to drawing circles in the dust.

CHAPTER 11

Tuesday was a sorry repetition of the first day, and I didn't have the energy to feign interest in classes. That got me reprimanded and instructed to stop dreaming twice. I spent time thinking about what I had learned the night before. The fact that there were different kinds of telepaths was not news to me. I had always known that telepaths could be more or less powerful, but the diversity in the abilities I had seen in the crypt was a different story. I was happy when the day ended, and I could join the students streaming out of the building. I was walking pensively toward my bike, now my inseparable steed, when a touch on my arm stopped me, and I turned to see Emily. She had a worried look on her face.

"Emily, what's up?" I asked.

"Can we talk?"

"Sure," I said, "talk."

"Not here."

"Okay ..."

"Let's go to the back."

"The back" was a pretty nice place, a garden behind the school where we could sit and eat during breaks. Emily guided me to a stone bench in a shaded corner and sat down. Everybody had left by then; the place was dead silent, and so was Emily.

"This is very nice," I said, trying to get the conversation started, "but you didn't bring me here to enjoy the chirping of the birds."

"It's about Nate."

"Yes?" I said helpfully.

"I don't know where to start."

"The beginning, perhaps?"

Emily swallowed nervously. She seemed to have trouble expressing herself. For a moment, I considered reading her, but then I decided that it would be easier to let her say what she needed to unload. After a full minute, she spoke again.

"I hope you won't think I'm crazy ... because of what I'm going to say."

"I won't; promise."

"Sometimes," she started, then after another pause, she continued, "sometimes I know what people are thinking."

That was alarming. I needed to tread carefully here if what Emily was saying was what I thought she was saying.

"You mean that you are an intuitive person; I get it. That's a good thing."

"No, no. I mean that I *actually* know what other people are thinking. A person stands beside me, and we talk, and I have flashes of his thoughts. One day, one of the girls was telling me how nice my dress was, and I knew that she thought that I'm a snob and a bitch. She was smiling at me and thinking that!"

As if my life wasn't tricky enough right then, I also needed a repressed telepath on my hands with all that was going on. But in a way, I felt that this connected me to her. I remembered feeling pretty much the same when all the visions had started. My abilities spooked me, and I had a hard time finding ways to talk to my parents and friends about them. Still, we had a situation here, and I didn't need this to make it more complicated than it already was.

"Okay, I believe you, but why are you telling this to me?"

"Because I have nobody else to talk to. You remember that I came to you and wanted to befriend you. It wasn't because you're nice—I'm not saying you aren't—but because I felt something. I can't explain it; it's a kind of radiation coming from you. When I felt it, I knew that I wanted to be your friend and that you would understand."

"You're right, I'm your friend, and I understand. It's good that you got this off your chest. Your secret is safe with me."

"But that's not it. That's not the problem; Nate is."

"What about him?"

"When we were going out, I told him. He was looking at another girl, and I knew he was thinking about her and how much he wanted her. I let it slip out that I knew it, and he laughed at me. He said that I would say the same about every girl in the same room with us. He *laughed* at me, so I had to prove it to him, and I told him exactly what he was thinking of doing with her."

"And what happened then?"

"He stopped laughing, said that I was exaggerating things as always, but I could tell he was rattled."

"But that was last year, right? So why are you worried now?"

"Yesterday he came to my house. He said that he wants me back, that he loves me, and can't think of me being with somebody else. He said that seeing me flirt with other boys drives him crazy. I told him it was too late and that I knew he didn't truly love me anyway. I knew that, to him, I am an object, a prize, which is exactly what he was thinking right then. Then I said that I would never go back with him."

"That must have sent him ballistic."

"It did. He yelled at me that I was a freak and should be grateful that he was willing to have me back. Then he threatened that he would tell everybody that I was a weirdo unless I got back with him. He would warn them that nobody should get close to me because I would steal their thoughts. I don't know what to do."

Emily was crying buckets by then, and I searched my brain for the right thing to say.

"Stall him," I said at last.

"What good will it do?"

"It will, trust me. I'm going to help you."

"How?"

"Trust me," I said. "It's a bit complicated, but you're right that I understand you, more than you know, so I'm going to fix this for you."

For the first time, Emily managed a smile.

"Really?"

"Really."

"I knew that I was right to come to you. So what do I do now?"

"You were right. Now blow your nose, put some glow on your face, and go tell Nate that he's always been the love of your life, and you want him back so much that it hurts."

"I hate him!"

"I know, but it's only for a little while, believe me."

"I do, and I don't know how to thank you."

We got up, and Emily hugged me. She was warm and smelled good. I had no trouble seeing why Nate wanted her back so much. I hadn't been around many people my age for a long time, so no wonder that I was getting frequent impure thoughts about some of them. But it was not the right time to give in to temptation.

Emily walked back with me to my bike, and then she got into her car, a small, red beetle-like thing, and we said goodbye. I pedaled without paying enough attention to the road and almost fell into a ditch, so engrossed I was in my thoughts. I wondered, is it my presence that makes everything more complicated than it should be, or is it fate that likes to play games with me?

CHAPTER 12

W hat do you do when you feel overwhelmed and unsure of your next step? You turn to a person that you trust and whose judgment you value if you have one. I searched my head for an answer to the question of who could be my pick here. Only a week before—it felt like a year, but in reality, it was less than a week—I would have spoken with Liv about it without thinking twice. But it was a week and a phone call later, so I couldn't. I rummaged my brain for an answer, but I knew that the first thought that had popped up in my mind was the correct one: ESA15.

ESA15 was not only the man who had taken me away from my family and trained me to become a remote viewer, but he had become the only person I knew who had the authority needed to make me take his advice seriously. I had learned to trust him after he enrolled me in the Remote Viewing Program, although there were times when I truly hated him for his strict training and lack of flexibility. A few months back, after the immediate danger to me from an executive gone mad and rogue had passed, ESA15 had cornered me and made me memorize a phone number. The fact that I ended up killing that executive was what made the danger pass, by the way, but it could have turned out to be the other way around.

"What do I need this number for, exactly?" I had asked.

"I hope you never will, but I want you to have it," ESA15 had answered. "This is my private, fully secure number that nobody can tap into. If you ever are in danger and need to speak with me, that's the number to call."

So if I was going to call anybody, ESA15 was my best and only option. It was a dilemma because he worked in government and was a straight arrow. By telling him too much, I might be giving myself away and putting myself and others in danger. But I hadn't forgotten that he had stood by me when I needed it and that his actions had a lot to do with the fact that I was still breathing.

I did all that reasoning while pedaling toward home, and when I reached that conclusion, I changed course toward the town center. The café where Emily and I had had our salad had a public telephone. I hadn't seen one of those in ages, but luckily small towns still had them. I walked in, ordered a soda, and went straight to it. I had ESA15's phone number etched in my brain—I have a knack for remembering numbers. I dialed it. It rang several times, and I was about to hang up when ESA15 picked up.

"Tessa, what's the problem?" he asked in his usual matter-of-fact way.

"Who said there is a problem?" I asked. Now that I had him on the line, I wasn't entirely sure that I should be telling him.

"Save us time. You have no business calling this number if you're not in real trouble."

"Can I speak freely?"

"A hundred percent."

"I think I'm being set up. I believe that a task force operates to kill every telepath it can find and has already killed a few. That's all I can say over the phone, secure or not."

"I'll come and see you. Let me check out a few things first. Where are you?"

I gave him the low-down as quickly as I could, and he remained silent for a few seconds.

"Can you get away from your present home tonight around ten?"

"Yes, I'll make up some social event. My dud parents know that I have to go to those to be effective."

"Good. I'm looking at the Google view of the town right now. Meet me at ten at the church."

"I'll be there," I said, and then he hung up.

There was something else that I had to do. I closed my eyes, pictured Jamie's face, and searched for him. In a split second, I reached him.

Jamie, I said, *we need to meet urgently, all of us, and that includes your father.*

What's the matter? he asked.

I can't explain right now; too complicated. I need you to fake an event, a party, something I can attend tonight around eight. Not at the crypt.

Well, that means that it will have to be my father's birthday all over again. We are throwing him a surprise party with BBQ in our backyard. Good enough for you?

Perfect! I'll be there with bells on.

That was the good part of all this. Jamie made me smile no matter what kind of danger I was in. I had to guard against it. He, falling in love with me, was one kind of problem, but me falling for him would be a trouble of an altogether different magnitude.

My "parents" weren't thrilled that I was going out again that evening, but they didn't have the authority to stop me. After all, I was the operative in the mission; they were only my cover story. I rejected Dad's suggestion that I should again wear the ghastly watch he had talked me into wearing the night of the bonfire. I knew he meant well, but there was a limit to what I was prepared to do to make him happy.

"If anything bad happens to me and they find me dead in a ditch, I don't want them to see that watch on me," I said, leaving no doubt about my decision.

"It's for your safety, you know. In case you need it."

"First of all, I'm going to a barbeque, not into a lair of murderous drug dealers, and second, I cannot hurt my social status by wearing that watch. If girls of my class see it, they'll stop inviting me, and then how will I do my job?"

"Still ..."

"No," I said and walked out.

Now that I had become familiar with the road to Jamie's house, it seemed shorter. Maybe it was because I pedaled more vigorously than usual; anyway, I arrived a few minutes before eight. Tracy was waiting for me and took me to the back door, which opened into a lovely garden that I hadn't seen when I visited before. Jamie had set the barbeque far from the house, where the garden merged into an open field.

"It's a bit far from the house," Tracy said at the door, "but Father is always worried about fire hazards, and we want him to feel comfortable tonight."

Bright girl, I pushed a thought to her.

Just so that if anybody's listening, he won't wonder why we put the BBQ so far away from the house—Jamie's idea.

Bright boy, too, I said.

The meat was cooking. Thomas had arrived, and Tracy went to fetch her father. The time had come to talk seriously.

"So, what was so urgent that we had to come up with this charade?" Nolan asked. "This is the third birthday party that my kids have thrown for me this year, and someone may take notice."

"I'm sorry about it, but we have a situation," I said.

I started by telling them about Emily, and then I told them about ESA15 without getting into too many details.

"You told a government high-brass about us? Are you crazy?" Thomas spurted.

"Not about you; I'm not stupid. I told him about the task force that kills telepaths. He and I go back a long way, and I trust him. I will meet him face to face later tonight, and I won't tell him about you, don't worry."

"But what good will get him involved do?" Tracy asked.

"You don't know him. Having him in my corner is important. He knows things and may help us. He's helped me against other government people before."

"But what about Emily?" Jamie asked.

"I hoped you would come up with an idea," I said. "I have a notion of where this should be going, but I'd rather hear you first."

"Kids," said Nolan, who so far had remained silent, "I feel that our time is running out. We must organize to leave. As you know, I have made plans for a contingency like this when the government would get too close ... again," he said, speaking with sadness in his voice. "I knew this time would come, although I hoped it wouldn't for at least one more year so you could finish school. Besides, we were comfortable here, but that's how it is."

"School is overrated," I said. "I haven't finished school and don't miss it a bit. And Nolan, you don't know how glad I am to hear you say that. I was afraid that you might not want to leave."

"I don't want to, but we have to. I'll make my final preparations. I need to get in touch with Mark. And you, Tessa, will come with us, right?"

I had pushed that thought into a far corner of my mind, but I knew I had to leave with them. My life as an ESA agent was coming to an end one way or another, and since I only had two alternatives, I definitely preferred leaving to getting killed.

"Yes, of course, and Emily too."

"Emily?" Nolan seemed perplexed. "She's not a real telepath; she only has flashes."

"Yes, but those flashes may evolve into something else as it happened to me. When the government picked me up, I wasn't much better than she."

"Emily is a bitch," Thomas spurted, "and she'll put us in danger. She can stay, and good luck to her. She's not one of us."

"If she isn't coming, I'm staying too," I said, earning a poisonous look from Thomas.

Atta girl! Came the thought from Tracy, and I smiled warmly at her.

"That's settled then," said Nolan, "Emily is coming. She's in your care, Tessa, okay? We have enough fish to fry without spending energy to bring her on board."

"I'll take care of that," I said.

"Now, let's eat," said Jamie. "The meat is ready."

CHAPTER 13

When I got to the church, I stopped for a moment in the street lights' safety before stepping into the darkness that surrounded the building. When I said that I trusted ESA15, I wasn't being exactly precise—I trusted him to a point. I thought it was improbable that he had brought an army of assassins to get rid of me—but unlikely does not equal impossible. I opened my mind and probed the surroundings. That is something else that I should explain. I can read people who are far away, but if I had no control over my reading radius, I would go mad with the background noise that millions of people generate. So when I want to contact a specific person, I know how to "channel" into him or her with surgical precision. Then, I can reach their mind with little or no background noise.

In contrast, when I don't have someone specific in mind, I can open my mind to whoever is around but limit my search radius. How do I do that? Hell, I wish I knew. I simply say to myself that I need to do this, and it's done.

So I opened my mind to thoughts nearby, and the only one I sensed was ESA15's. As a result, I felt safe and walked up to the church. He was standing by the door and greeted me with his customary, "You're late."

"Thirty seconds by my watch," I said.

"Late is late; not a question of how much," he said, taking a deep breath. "How are you doing, Tessa?" he continued in a softer tone.

"Not so hot, as you can imagine, or I wouldn't have dragged you over here. I have a lot of things to consider and decisions to make."

"You didn't drag me here; I volunteered," he said, being a stickler for precision as always, "and it's a good thing you contacted me. You're treading in a snake pit."

"I knew that you would put my mind at ease," I said, spicing that up with a smirk.

"This is no time for wisecracks, Tessa; this is serious."

"I know; I'm sorry."

"I had to call in a few favors and break into a few files I had no business looking at to get a clue of what's going on here, and that's all I got: an inkling. What I know is worrisome enough, but hopefully, it is also useful and may be instrumental in saving your ass."

"I appreciate it ..."

"Yes, now listen. You were absolutely right. There is a task force going after telepaths. I don't know who authorized it and whether it is authorized at all, but it operates and has been operating for at least seven years. It is top secret and doesn't appear in the official department documentation. The task force is small—I don't know its exact strength, but it appears to have between five and ten killers. The head of the task force is a ruthless brute known as Schmidt, first name unknown."

"Is there anything you can do to stop this Schmidt person? After all, you're high up in the chain of command."

"You can't stop someone who doesn't exist, and Schmidt doesn't exist, at least officially. But maybe you can."

"How can I find him?"

"He's easier to find than you would think. Right now, he's working under the assumed name of Robert Jones."

It took me a moment to realize what I had just heard. Robert Jones was Bob, and Bob was ... "Dad!"

"Holy shit! Shit! Shit! Shit!"

"Yes, that's disturbing, but don't get too excited—he doesn't know that you know, and until he does, you're safe."

"And to think that I had started to like him. I thought he was trying to protect me! That sucks a million!"

"That's the snake I was talking about."

"What can I do?" My head was spinning.

"Well, as I see it, you have two options: The first, which is the one I would choose, is to kill him. You've done that before. The other one is for you to disappear until the situation resolves itself."

"The one I killed was coming to kill me, which made it self-defense. And besides, who says that if I kill this Schmidt, someone else won't take his place?"

"I would count this as self-defense too, but that's your call. You're right, though; if he's done away with, some other louse will likely take his place, so that wouldn't be a final solution, merely a reprieve."

"He must be a self-confident bastard not to be worried that I might read him and find out."

"First of all, he must be assuming that you suspect nothing and have no reason to probe him. Besides, one of the documents I managed to read tells an interesting tale about the mind-shielding training he took. It teaches you to think intensely about some neutral topic when you are around someone who may want to read you. That thought is so noisy that it is difficult for anybody to dig deeper and get any useful information. The Soviets developed the technique, and that's where he learned it. Apparently, now he teaches that technique."

"The bastard! He fed me crap about gardening and local newspaper headlines."

"Yes, that would be it."

A disturbing thought crossed my mind, and I had to ask.

"Is Mary in on any of this? After all, she runs the Extra-Sensory Unit."

"I don't think so. I'm not even sure that she'll be around for long. I got a feeling that she has fallen from grace with the powers that be. Concerning your situation, I think she's being manipulated and doesn't know that the whole story they made up to send you here, about the non-existent leak and all that, was a fabrication. But you can't talk to her about any of it. She wouldn't endanger herself or her career for you."

"But you would ..."

"I am doing it. Despite you being an awful brat, I've always looked upon you as a daughter. You know that, although we never spoke in those terms. It's not a good way to maintain the distance we need in our line of business. But we face an extreme situation, and I'm telling you this now because I want you to be confident that you can count on me."

"To say that I appreciate it doesn't even start to describe it." I choked a little on the last words and turned my face to hide the moisture in my eyes. It felt like I finally had a father on whom I could rely. My real one is a dear, but I could never talk to him about any of this. "I can't tell you how much it means to me. I feel awful about calling you names in the past and being a pest to you."

"Let's not speak about this anymore," he said brusquely. "Let's talk about what you are going to do."

"Which is?"

"Disappear and lie low for as long as needed. I will need to come up with an airtight plan. I haven't had the time to think of a good one yet."

"You don't need to; I have that covered."

"How?"

"I think it's best if I tell you no more. It might put you and other people in more danger."

"All right, as long as you manage by yourself, but if you don't, you have my number. I'm leaving now. My official travel plan says I'm three hundred miles from here. I need to get there in time to order breakfast from room service to make it check out."

I don't know what got into me. I had always respected ESA15, but he had always treated me like an agent that needed keeping in line, which had maintained a frozen gap between us. But now, I automatically took another step toward him and hugged him as hard as I could, and I'm a strong girl. I felt his hands on my shoulder blades, applying a little, almost timid pressure in return for a moment, and when he removed his hands, I took a step back.

"Thank you," I said, and damn it if I didn't have to hide a tear from him this time.

"You're welcome, but don't do that again," he said. Then he turned away, and the darkness swallowed him.

CHAPTER 14

Back at Jamie's house that evening, Nolan had shown himself for the practical person he was.

"We need to avoid drawing attention to ourselves, so until everything is ready for us to leave, you must keep going as if nothing has happened. Tomorrow you are going to school as usual and playing the good students, okay?" he had instructed us.

We all nodded in assent. Clearly, that was what we needed to do. But now, there was one more factor to be considered, and Nolan had to know about it.

Jamie, I pushed the thought in his direction.

Tessa ... you can't sleep either, right? Are you excited? I'm so glad that we will be leaving together. This is going to be a real adventure—

Hold on, I checked him; *you need to hear this. I just found out that Bob, the one who plays the role of my father here, he's the head of the snake.*

What do you mean?

He heads the task force that's hunting us. He's dangerous, and he's here. You need to tell your father, and you need to tell him right now.

Jamie was silent for a long time, apparently digesting the news.

But that means that you're in danger!

That means that we all are in danger. Tell your father, tell him now.

I'll wake him up, Jamie said, and even though a mental voice is not exactly like an actual voice, it wasn't hard to hear the anxiety in it.

I can go to sleep at the snap of a finger, which is another one of my knacks, but that night falling asleep took a long time. I had a dream in which Bob was chasing me with a big, whacking knife, which is unusual for me since, as a rule, I am a dreamless sleeper, and I'm not prone to nightmares. True, in the dream, he was scaly and green all over, which helped me realize that I was having a lucid dream, but I woke up feeling unrested.

Breakfast was the worst part of that morning because I needed to be my usual breezy self, which was the opposite of how I felt. I am only a mediocre liar, so apparently, something in my demeanor wasn't exactly right.

"What's the matter with you, honey?" Mom asked, "Aren't you feeling well?"

"Yup. Something must have been wrong with the meat I ate yesterday. I had a stomach ache all night and didn't sleep well, but I'm okay now, thanks for asking."

"Do you want me to drive you to school?" asked Dad.

"No, thank you. I'll ride my bike. The fresh air will do me good."

Being an alleged stomach sufferer, I skipped the eggs and

limited myself to a slice of bread with honey and a cup of tea, and then I said a hurried "bye" and left.

I suffered through a double English lesson and boring geography, which took us to the lunch break. I had a sandwich with me, which I planned to eat in peace outside, but Tracy stopped me in the corridor. To an outsider, our conversation had to do with school, but below the surface, this is what went on:

Jamie told me. My God! You must be scared stiff.

I'm not scared, but I'm worried. I'm okay.

I wanted to tell you that I'm here if you need to talk or if you feel that the pressure is too much.

Don't worry; I'll keep my cool. Now I have to go and eat my sandwich. I virtually skipped breakfast today; I wanted to get out of the house as quickly as possible.

Tracy nodded, and I moved on. Outside, I found a nice, shaded seat at the edge of the front lawn and sat down to eat. I had finished eating and had got up to go back into the school building when something I saw far away by the school entrance made me freeze. I squinted to make sure that I was really seeing Bob and Thomas talking, and there they were. I strode as fast as I could without looking as if I was hurrying. I had to know what that was about and stop anything that was happening, no matter what. But by the time I reached the entrance, Thomas had left, and Bob was standing there alone.

"What are you doing here?" I asked.

"Oh, hi, Alex. I'm paying a visit to your principal."

"Why?"

"Because," Bob said, lowering his voice to a bare whisper, "I expect that Miss Wharburg would find it strange if a dedicated father like myself didn't take an interest in how his daughter was doing."

"You didn't tell me that you were planning to come this morning."

"I thought about it later. I don't have much real work to do anyway, and this visit helps me pass the time."

"Okay. And what did that boy want?"

"Which boy?"

"The one with whom you were talking just now."

"That one? He didn't want anything. I asked for directions to Miss Wharburg's office. Why?"

"Oh, it's just that I know him, and I think he's planning on hitting on me. Doesn't matter, go talk to Miss Wharburg, but I warn you, she's a bore, and she'll keep you forever, complaining about the way I dress."

I waited for Bob to walk into the building, and then I went to look for Thomas. I found him near the lockers and dragged him to a quiet corner.

"What was that about?" I asked point-blank.

"What was what about?"

"You talking to my father out there."

"Was that your father? I didn't know him. He asked for directions to Miss Wharburg's office, that's all."

Thomas was a telepath, so I couldn't read him without him knowing what I was doing, but the telemoticon I got from him told me he was lying. I didn't know what was going on, but I decided not to confront him, not yet, at least.

"Okay, a coincidence, then, but stay away from him in the future; you know he's government."

"Sure, but I couldn't very well refuse to tell him where to go, even if I had known who he was."

"You're right, no harm done," I said, but sure as hell, I did not believe it.

CHAPTER 15

Nolan had told us to be patient because some things needed organizing, which took time. But with each day that passed, we became more fretful, to the point when we had to make a real effort to hide it. It killed me that we didn't know how long we had to wait. Besides, I couldn't keep my suspicion about Thomas and his talking to Bob to myself any longer. I had decided to wait 24 hours before talking to Jamie and Tracy, but now I wondered whether I shouldn't have told them immediately. But what did I have to say? That I found his telemoticon suspicious when I spoke with him? Thomas was a lifelong friend of Jamie's, and I couldn't go about making unsupported accusations about him. Still, our lives hung on being cautious and truthful, and I had kept what could be critical information from the others. What a mess!

However, as messes do, this one kind of resolved itself when Nate approached me during a school break.

"Alex, do you have a moment?"

"What can I do for you, Nate?" I asked, making sure that the vibe I was sending said, "No, I'm not going out with you."

"Emily says that you two have become best friends ..."

"We have."

"So perhaps you can tell me what's going on with her and where she is?"

"What do you mean?"

"Look, you know that Emily and I are back together ..."

"I knew that she wanted to. She told me that she never stopped loving you and missed you, but I didn't know that you had patched things up already."

"We did ... actually, she came to me, and I agreed to take her back. I'm sorry if this bums you out."

You arrogant idiot, I thought, but I said, "So what's the problem?"

"I don't know where she is. She didn't show up at school this morning. We had a rehearsal for the school play that she and I volunteered for only yesterday, and she didn't show, plus she isn't answering her cellphone."

"Maybe she's sick. Try her home."

"I did try. Her mom said that she's in school, only she isn't."

"Oh. My God, she must be worried sick."

"I didn't tell her; you think I'm stupid? I don't know where Emily went, but if she didn't want her mother to know, I'm not the one to tell her."

"Good call. I don't know where she is either, I swear, but as soon as I see her, I'll tell her to call you, okay?"

"You do that. And tell her I'm pissed off that she isn't keeping in touch," Nate said and went on to ask other people.

I leaned against a nearby tree. I had to concentrate. I brought Emily's face before my mental eyes, and in a second, I was in her head. She was in a windowless room, a basement of sorts, and was crying. I realized that she was a prisoner and, obviously, was in danger. I didn't know right then what her kidnapping had to do with anything, but I had a strong feeling that it was somehow connected with us.

Waiting for the end of the school day was torture, but Emily didn't seem to be in immediate danger. I checked on her several times, and the last time I did, she had fallen asleep, exhausted from crying her eyes out. Meanwhile, I agreed with the others to meet outside as soon as school was over.

The city had built our school far from other city buildings. It had rolling grass fields all around and a beautiful copse of long-leafed trees, the name of which I don't know, and I don't care to know. The copse grew beside the road leading to the school, some 500 yards away. I took Jamie, Tracy, and Thomas there, ignoring their questions about what I had in mind and why the hell we were going into the woods. All I said was that we needed a safe place to talk where nobody could eavesdrop.

"So, what's going on?" Jamie asked as soon as we got there and had walked a reasonable distance from the road into the thicket.

"Perhaps Thomas will tell us," I said, and everybody turned to look at him.

"I have nothing to say. I don't know what you want," said Thomas, looking and sounding openly defensive.

"I'll tell you what," I said to the others. "Yesterday, I saw Thomas talking with the devil, more precisely, Bob. When I asked him, he gave me a bullshit answer about giving Bob directions to Miss Wharburg's office. Now Nate tells me that Emily has disappeared. I looked for her and got into her head, and imagine what? She's being held prisoner in some kind of basement. Now don't tell me this has nothing to do with you, Thomas, 'cause I'm not buying it."

"What's going on, Tommy?" Jamie asked. The pained look on his face was hard to watch. Betrayals are hard to bear when they come from people close to you. I should know.

Thomas swallowed twice in rapid succession and let his gaze move from me to Jamie, then to Tracy, and then to the floor. He tried to speak but choked, then swallowed some more before speaking.

"I was trying to protect you," he said at last.

"Doing what?" Jamie asked.

"Look, this man who calls himself Bob came to me at school. He said that he knew that I knew he was a government agent. He said he had heard bits and pieces of our conversation that first night in the crypt. It was garbled because of the stone walls and almost no reception, but the little bit he had heard had been enough to identify me."

"The watch! The one the bastard made me wear that night. It must contain a transmitter. How stupid I was; I'm so sorry; I put everybody in danger."

"You didn't know it; it's not your fault," Tracy said softly.

"It's my fault that I was stupid. I'm truly sorry. So what else did Bob say?"

"He knew there were others but didn't know who they were. I told him that there were only two others, and I think he bought it. I told him that one was Tessa because he knew that already anyway, but I had to give him another one. He said that if I gave him another one, he would give me impunity and leave me alone, so I gave him Emily. Tessa had just told us that she is a telepath, and she isn't one of us, so I gave her to him. I'm sorry I didn't tell you, but I was scared."

Thomas was almost crying now, but that didn't make me feel sorry for him.

"You stupid idiot!" I said. "If I was stupid once, you've been stupid enough to last a lifetime. Did you really think that he would let you live? He needs to kill us all; he's simply biding his time, finding a clean way of doing it, or maybe he hopes to get more information from you first."

"We need to talk to Father," Tracy said, "and now is not soon enough."

"You're right," I said, "and we need to plan how to get Emily back and take her with us."

"But she's not one of us," Jamie objected, "and we don't know if she even will want to come with us. She may want to stay put with her family."

"That's too bad," I said, speaking slowly, "because I already told you once that if she's not coming with us, I'm not going either, and I meant it."

CHAPTER 16

"I got word from Mark that we can get away, so this is the plan," Nolan said. "We have two SUVs. I will drive one, and Sandie, Thomas's mother, will drive the other. Jamie and Tessa will ride with me, and Thomas and Tracy will go with Sandie. All clear?"

"And where is Emily going to be?" I asked.

It was late afternoon, and we were once again in Nolan's backyard, far away from the house.

"I don't know, Tessa. We'll see when we get there. Meanwhile, it's important that you all know our initial itinerary and where we will meet in case we get separated. I'll have maps marked for you when we leave. And then Tracy and Jamie can maintain contact if anything goes wrong with the road and the meeting points. I have already made plans with Sandie. The SUVs are hidden in the abandoned barn on that side road that branches out to the left, one mile from here. We are leaving at 7 PM sharp tomorrow evening. That gives us 24 hours to organize and think about Emily. Speaking of which, wouldn't her mother be calling the police by now?"

"No, Tessa asked me to call Emily's mother," Tracy said. "I

called her and asked to speak with Emily. Her mother said that she had sent her a text message. She was staying with a friend to study and prepare for a test tomorrow."

"Which we know she didn't send," I pointed out. "That means that Bob—Schmidt—doesn't want the alarm to be raised with us yet, which also means that he has some plan that he still needs time for. That's good."

"Do you have any idea where he's holding Emily?" Nolan asked.

"None, but it has to be nearby. Later tonight, I'll get into Emily's head and try to find out what she knows about it. What's clear is that we need to find her and free her quickly before anything bad happens to her."

"If Schmidt is keeping her prisoner, it means that he needs her for something. He may be planning to use her as bait for us. That also means we must be very careful," Jamie pointed out.

"And you all need to go to school tomorrow and behave as usual," said Nolan. "I have a hunch that Schmidt is waiting to see who behaves differently after Emily disappeared, and that person may be who he's looking for."

"I'll push updates to you every half hour or so, Dad, so you know we are doing okay."

"Yes, do that. It gives me a headache after a while when you push messages to me, but it's better than worrying all morning."

It took quite an effort for me to behave normally at home that night. It started with Bob getting all uncharacteristically chatty, which I didn't like a bit.

"How about your progress report?" he asked over dessert. I

had decided not to skip dinner at home for the sake of regular appearances.

"What about it?"

"Aren't you supposed to prepare a weekly one?"

"I am, but why is that any problem of yours? I count the week from when school began, so it's not due until Sunday."

"All right, I'm trying to be helpful; no need to bite my head off."

"I'm not—biting your head off, I mean. It's just that progress is slow, and I'm a bit frustrated. I hate to send in reports saying I have accomplished zilch."

"I can understand that. Well, dinner was delicious, honey," Bob said, getting a pleased smile in return from Barb. "You're fattening me. I need to take a walk and burn some of those calories off," he added and walked out.

"What about you, sweetie? Do you want to watch 'Wheel of Fortune' with me?"

"Thanks, but I'm too tired. I'll go up to my room and turn in early."

I needed to think fast. Bob was likely going to Emily, and it could be my opportunity to learn where he was keeping her. Up in my room, I opened the window and gazed out. In the distance, I saw Bob walking away. For a moment, I toyed with the idea of sliding down the water pipe that ran near my window, but I rejected it. First, the pipe looked old and rusty, and I doubted it would hold my weight. Second, I wasn't keen on breaking my neck, climbing down or up it, and, besides, the noise would bring Barb running out of the house in a heartbeat. No, I was stuck.

Then I saw the solution. Sitting outside his house was the old wino who had spoken to me the day I arrived. He had an almost empty bottle of liquor by his side and was muttering to himself; God knew what. I gazed at him intensely, and in a moment, I was in his head, and what a dirty, fuzzy head it was. The taste of the cheap liquor and rising bile in his mouth made me gag a little, but

I managed to ignore it. I took possession of his body and made him stand up. He only offered a weak resistance, and soon I had complete control. I made him walk after Bob. His gait was a bit wobbly, and I had to make an effort to make him walk faster and less noisily than was his natural disposition. He was the perfect vehicle for me, though—nobody would have suspected he was anything other than a drunkard walking about aimlessly.

I was relieved when, after two minutes, I spotted Bob in the distance. He entered a house that looked pretty much like ours, except that it had no name sign on the door and no lights on until he walked in. I slowed my walk and passed by the house, taking a position at a bend in the road from which I could see it. About ten minutes passed before the lights went off again, and Bob came out. He walked back toward our home, and I followed him to make sure that he wasn't going anywhere else. He reached home and walked in. From my room, I heard him talking with Barb, laughing a bit, and then only the TV.

Meanwhile, my wino neighbor had wobbled back to his house. I made him sit in his garden chair like before and pick up the bottle. As a last gesture, I made him take a swig, which almost made me puke, and then I let go of him. When he got sober again, if ever, he would attribute our little trip to the bottle if he even remembered it.

Now I knew where Emily was, and all that remained was to think of a way to get her out of there. I smiled to myself, thinking how smart Bob thought he was. He didn't know who he was up against.

I still locked my door, though. I knew I wouldn't be able to sleep otherwise, but I hated that it made me feel vulnerable.

CHAPTER 17

The following day, I pedaled to school as usual. I parked my bike at the usual place and quickly walked into the nearby thicket that had become our meeting place.

Where are you? I pushed a message to Jamie.

"Right behind you," came his voice, and I turned around.

Jamie's face was severe, and I could feel how tense he was without even trying.

"Good," I said, "let's get going."

"Wait a minute. What type of man is this Schmidt-Bob? I mean, if he shows up while we are there, it may be dangerous, yes? I'm asking because I never saw him. Shouldn't we have a weapon or something with us?"

"Bob is dangerous, but I'll deal with him if he shows up."

I had handled much more dangerous goons before, and I wasn't worried that I couldn't take Bob. What I was worried about was seeing how fidgety Jamie was. I didn't need him to break down in the middle of things.

"Oh, if you're sure ..."

"I'm sure, but are you sure you want to come? I can go alone if you don't feel up to it."

"Of course, I'm up to it," Jamie spurted angrily. "What kind of human being would I be if I let you go alone?"

"All right. I'm sorry. Let's go."

We walked side by side in the fields, Jamie in a hurt silence that I preferred not to break. We stayed a little away from the road to be ready to lie down and hide if a car drove by. Luckily, we ran into no vehicles, and nobody saw us. At that hour in the morning, the place was as good as a ghost town, which was perfect for us. We managed to get to the house where Emily was kept prisoner without being spotted and having silly questions asked us, like why we were not in school, for example. I knew that I had hurt Jamie's feelings—the vibe that came from him was unmistakable—and I made a mental note to make it up to him later. But it was time he realized that with me, you will always know what I think and that I don't put filters on my mouth when I tell it to you.

When we reached the house, I opened my mind for a second and got a vision of Emily, frightened in that basement.

"She's here," I said.

"How do we get in?" asked Jamie.

Well, hell, I hadn't thought of that little detail. The door was locked, and we didn't have the key. It wasn't much of a door, though, a wood-paneled thing that looked rather rotten at the edges, and the doorframe seemed to keep it in place for a bet. I looked around and saw a shovel lying there in what once had been a garden but now was a field of thorns.

"We break the door. Here, take that shovel and jam it between the door and the frame near the lock."

Without arguing, Jamie did it, and in a second, the door was open.

"Wow, that was a bright idea," he said.

"And a great performance," I said, smiling at him. His success with the door had bucked him up a little, and I wanted to contribute to strengthening his self-esteem. "Come in and bring the shovel. We may need it to open the basement door."

But when we got to the basement, a bad surprise awaited us. The door was made of heavy metal, and the frame was steel, nothing that our shovel could handle. But at least we could cheer Emily up a little.

"Emily, can you hear me? It's me, Alex, and Jamie is with me. We'll get you out of there."

"Alex? Please open this door and let me out," Emily's anguished voice filtered through the door.

"Yes, we are working on it; a little patience. You'll be out in no time," I yelled, although I had no idea how to do it right then.

"I don't think so," said Bob from behind us, waving a big pistol to support his statement.

"Well, well, well, my method is working," said Bob, speaking smugly. "I knew that keeping this girl here would attract you like vermin to honey. So here's another one I didn't know about," he said, gazing at Jamie. "And you, Tessa, you thought I didn't know you were conniving with them to make our mission fail?"

At that point, I was thoroughly pissed off, and when I am, I become nasty.

"First of all, 'Dad,' vermin are not attracted to honey for your information. You were thinking of flies. And then, I will need that gun."

It had only taken me a second to get into his head, and as I spoke, he was already immobilized. I got hold of the gun and made him release his grip. I wasn't controlling his facial muscles because his terrified expression was too good to miss.

"You're amazing," Jessie murmured.

"Yes, I am, and now please be amazing too and fish into his pockets. He must have a key to this door."

Jamie approached him and searched his pockets. Soon his hand came out with a ring with two keys. Bob was taller than Jamie, so he tilted his head up a little to gaze at Bob's face. He stared at him for a few seconds, then tried the keys on the door. At the second attempt, the lock turned, and Jamie pushed the door open. Emily came rushing out but stopped in her tracks, seeing Bob there.

"He, he ..." she started to say but ended up speechless.

"Don't worry about him; he's harmless," I said. "I'm controlling him."

"But how?" she managed to say.

"It's too complicated to explain now. I just do, look."

I brought Bob down to his knees and made him lie face down on the floor. Jamie went to stand, straddling his body.

Emily's jaw dropped, and she gazed at me, either in awe or in fear; I couldn't say which.

"The only problem now is that I don't know what we are going to do with him," I said.

"I know what," said Jamie.

He was still holding the shovel in his hand. Gripping it in both hands, he raised it, and before I could speak, he brought it down on the back of Bob's neck, and that's the last thing I remember seeing before I passed out.

CHAPTER 18

When I came to, the first thing I felt was that my face was wet. Someone had sprinkled water on it in an attempt to wake me up. Besides, Jamie's face was pressed to mine, and he had big tears running down his cheeks and wetting me some more. His face lit up as soon as he saw me open my eyes.

"You're back!" he said.

I looked around, taking in the scene. Emily stood a bit aside, clearly in shock, and Bob's partly decapitated body lay in a large pool of blood. His head, still attached to the body by some tissue, had rotated at an unnatural angle.

"You dropped there without a word. I was so scared. I couldn't understand what was happening," Jamie said, his voice breaking.

"What was happening was that you killed Bob while I was in his head. You could have killed me too, you moron!"

I felt too nauseous to give expression to my fully enraged self, so I postponed it to a time when I could give him a piece of my mind at leisure. Right then, I was busy regaining my senses. Although it had been an unpleasant experience, there was a positive angle to it: now I knew that if I happened to be in someone's head when they died, it would probably not kill me. I had wondered about that, and knowing how things turned out was a relief.

"I'm so sorry! I had no idea that this would happen."

"They call this 'thinking,' Jamie, thinking *before* you act. What got into you anyway? Why did you do it?"

Jamie pursed his lips as if debating whether to explain himself.

"You remember that I told you about Anne and what happened to her?" he finally said.

"Yes. I remember."

"The last thing I saw through her eyes was a face, that of the man who killed her—"

Jamie choked a little and didn't seem able to go on speaking, but I had understood.

"And that face was Bob's, right?"

Jamie nodded, still too emotional to speak.

"Then you had all the reasons to kill him, and I'm glad you did."

"I never killed anybody ... even not a cockroach, but I'm not sorry I killed him. I thought I might end up feeling guilty about it but decided to do it anyway," said Jamie, sounding surprised with himself.

"But what ... how ...," Emily tried to ask.

I was sitting on the floor and still a bit nauseous. My head spun every time I moved it, but I knew we had no time to lose, so I got up anyway.

"Come, Emily, let's go to another room where we can speak quietly. There is a lot we need to tell you and very little time to tell it."

I thought that Emily had taken it rather well, everything considered. Maybe it was because she was still in a kind of stupor, and reality had not yet caught up with her. I don't think that she realized that getting away with us meant permanently abandoning her family and the life she was used to. But she would realize that soon enough.

We hoped that killing Bob had bought us some more time. We had to stick to the plan and show up at school as if nothing had happened. We walked back to school. It was a brisk walk of fifteen minutes, but now it took us almost twice as long because we walked in the fields, trying to hide from the road.

"I can't go inside like this," Emily complained, "not the way I look. My clothes are all creased, and I don't smell good."

"Emily," I said, "you could stay in that basement and in your clothes for another week and still look better than most girls here. You'll have to tough it out for once."

It wasn't true, of course. Emily looked like someone who had slept in her clothes, and she did smell a little, but that was the least of her troubles. It was just that she hadn't realized it yet.

We reached school minutes before the end of the break leading into the third hour—English—and hurried to class. Tracy and Thomas were waiting anxiously by the door, and when they saw that Emily was with us, they relaxed.

All good? Tracy pushed a question at me.

Marshmallow, I answered. It wasn't a good time to go into detail. I saw from his expression that Thomas had also received a quieting message from Jamie, and the five of us walked into the classroom. I was happy to see that Nate was not there.

Now that the rescue's immediate danger was behind us, I started to feel the tension that had accompanied it. My heart pounded, and to calm down, I needed to think that the world around us was kind of normal, even if only for a while. Strangely, listening to the teacher babbling about Lord Byron was relaxing.

Then, of course, an announcement came to disrupt it. It

wasn't given over the school system, which all it could do was emit unintelligible croaking sounds. It came from much louder and more effective loudspeakers. It shouted:

THIS IS AN EMERGENCY FEDERAL MARSHALL ANNOUNCEMENT. ALL STUDENTS AND TEACHERS MUST FILE OUT AND IDENTIFY THEMSELVES AT THE DOOR. ONLY THE FRONT DOOR IS OPEN; ALL OTHER EXITS ARE BLOCKED. COME TO THE FRONT DOOR NOW.

That's when I knew that we were in deep shit.

The announcement kept repeating itself, and our classmates got up and piled out of the door, chattering. In the corridor, students were pouring in from every classroom. I went to the window and looked. Police cars with flashing lights blocked the driveway, and a bunch of uniformed officers waited by the door for the first students who started to exit. I saw Barb holding a mike next to a police car. She no longer looked like a housewife, perhaps because she was wearing a bulletproof vest. Somehow, she had found out that Bob was dead and was coming after us.

The classroom was empty now but for the five of us. I didn't know the school building as well as the others and needed their help to figure out what to do. Only, as I was soon to learn, there wasn't much that we could do.

"They say that all exits are blocked. Do you have an idea how we can get out of here?" I asked, not expecting much of an answer.

"We could go to the roof," Thomas volunteered.

"And then what? There's no way off the roof," Jamie said in despair.

"Let's go to the music room," said Tracy. "I have an idea."

No matter how idiotic, I would have taken any idea since I had none, so we followed her. The corridor near our class was empty, and we ran to the music room. That room was pretty much a junk-yard, with all kinds of musical instruments lying around without any specific or logical order. The lighting was low, and I had wondered before why they didn't use stronger light bulbs, but perhaps it was to create a musical atmosphere. Tracy guided us to a corner that was home to an assembly of seven large string instruments. There was a cello, a contrabass, and other musical instruments that I could not name. She instructed us to stand beside them, crouching, holding one another tight.

"Do you mind telling us what the plan is?" I asked after complying. I usually give the benefit of the doubt to whoever is telling me to do something for my own good, hoping that they know what they're doing.

"Look, you remember what I showed you with the cherubs in the crypt? We'll do the same here."

"How?"

"The human eye can cancel images if it's fixed on something else. What I do is make whoever is looking at me concentrate on something else near me, and then he doesn't see me. He thinks that he has seen everything there is to see in my direction, but he has missed me."

"That's swell when it's only you, with your tiny, slim figure. But there are five of us here. How do you think this could work?"

"That's why I brought us to stand beside this heap of instruments. If I can make them concentrate on the middle of the heap, their eyes will miss what's in the periphery. We have to be completely silent. I can't cancel sounds as well as images, although I can mask them a little, but not all at the same time. It takes too much concentration."

"Well, I've no better idea, so let's hope yours works," I said, and right then, the door opened.

CHAPTER 19

I believe that I held my breath for the length of the inspection. A policeman came in, followed by Miss Wharburg.

"What's this place, Miss?" he asked.

"This is the music room, and, as you can see, it's empty. There is nowhere to hide, and nobody's here."

"I thought for a moment ... but no, you're right. It was just the light playing tricks on my eyes. All right, let's move on, but I need you to lock the door so nobody can come in here. The instructions the feds gave us are to leave every room of the school that we inspect sterile."

They left, closing and locking the door behind them.

"Woof!" I said, breathing again. "You're amazing, Tracy!"

"Enthusiasm aside," Jamie pointed out, "we are locked in. We haven't been found out yet, but how does that improve our situation?"

"We need to take things as they come, one at a time," said Tracy. "We figured out this one, and now we need to figure out the next. Speaking of which, Thomas, why are you so quiet? You could lend a hand here."

"I ... I'm ashamed and don't know what to say. I could have got Emily killed, and I'm so sorry."

"Got me killed? How?"

"It's a long story, no time to go into it now," I hastened to say. If there ever was a wrong time for apologizing and seeking absolution, that was that time. Thomas was proving to me, again, that he wasn't a bright boy. We would have to guard against any other stupid ideas he might come up with while flying for our lives. Only, so far, we were locked in a music room, not flying.

"No, I want to know," Emily insisted.

"Thomas told Bob, the man who kidnapped you, that you are a latent telepath. He thought that it would do you no harm and would save the rest of us from getting killed."

"So it was because of you ..."

"Yes, but it may have all been for nothing because if we don't get out of here, they'll find us in the end, and we will get killed. I'm sorry," I said, trying my best fatalistic tone to avoid scaring anybody, although they had to be scared enough without my help.

"You see, Emily," I explained, "our only crime is that we are a bit more sensitive than other people and have some extrasensory abilities. We haven't done anything wrong to anybody. They hunt all kids with special abilities, and they end up dead. They have decided to exterminate all of us simply because we are different from them."

Emily had started to cry silently, and now she wiped her eyes and gazed straight at me.

"If what you say is true, and you're not saying it to scare me, if it's true that we are going to die, I want to know. Tell me if we are."

"No, you are not," said a voice from behind a large organ propped against the wall. I knew that voice, and so did the others.

"Miss Wharburg!" we all cried in unison.

She emerged from behind the organ and came to stand before us.

"Poor things," she said, speaking compassionately. "I heard what you said, and I won't have it. Not one of my pupils will be harmed as long as I am the principal of this school."

"But how ... how did you know that we're here? And how did you get in here?"

"When I came into the room with that officer, I spotted you immediately, but um, I realized that he didn't see you, and when I fixed my gaze on something, you disappeared. I moved my eyes rapidly from side to side, and you reappeared. I couldn't understand how that was happening and why you were standing there like a group of statues. I didn't believe my eyes for a moment, but um, when he concluded that the room was empty, I decided to investigate."

"Thanks for not giving us away, Miss Wharburg," Emily said meekly.

"So I came the back way," Miss Wharburg continued. "I heard you speaking among yourselves and listened in. I had to make sure that you had committed no crime and weren't a danger to anyone. That woman, that federal marshal, said that dangerous terrorists were hiding in my school and had to be found before they killed anybody."

"Miss Wharburg, I swear—" Thomas started to say, but she cut him short.

"You don't need to swear. I heard you, and I know that you were telling the truth. I think that what the police are doing is disgraceful, and I won't allow it!" She spoke vehemently, and it was heartwarming.

"But how did you get in here?" I asked. I had hoped that she could lead us out. Obviously, a passage led to the music room, but if it came from another inner chamber, that wouldn't help us get away.

"This is an ancient building. Its foundations date back to the Civil War, and as you know, history is my passion. It used to be a monastery back then, and this school was built on the ruins of that monastery that was partially still standing. This room was part of the ancient building that was preserved. I found an old map that shows passages that the monks used to come and go. I kept it to myself because I didn't want the municipality to mess with the building. Besides, I wanted to explore it on my own, without having intruders come and tell me what I can or cannot study. One of those passages leads from behind a cupboard in my office into here, behind that organ."

"So, the best we can do is go from here to your office?" I asked.

"I said 'passages,' plural. You should pay attention. One passage is a long underground way that leads out into the fields behind the school building. It ends at a ruined structure that would have held a water tank once. That's where you need to go."

"I say we go there immediately," said Jamie, looking lively again.

"Yes, but we can't exit before the police have left," I pointed out. "It might be dangerous. We don't know how far they are looking and with what equipment they are watching. Before we go, you need to tell your father what's happening. They may go and look for him and Sandie once they figure out who's missing from school."

"It'll take them some time to do that," said Miss Wharburg, smiling. "I gave them last year's list of students tabulated in my handwriting, but um, even I can't read it sometimes."

"Miss Wharburg, you're great! You're awesome!" I said, and I meant it. "Anything I thought differently about you before, I'm taking back."

"Now it's time to go before anybody comes to look for me and wonders where I've disappeared," said Miss Wharburg. "This way to the passage," she added, pointing at the organ.

"I'm done telling Father," said Jamie.

"And what about me?" Emily asked.

"Now you're officially one of us," Thomas said. "Come."

CHAPTER 20

The underground passage was damp and dark, but for the little light that my cellphone made. It smelled of mice and decaying stuff. Still, I can't recall a place I wanted to get into more. Miss Wharburg had taken us to the tunnel entrance, where some passageways met, and had left us there. She made us promise that we would come to see her "when all this confusion is over," as she put it. She had also given each of us a bottle of water and some crackers, making us feel like we were about to go on a school trip. Then she had disappeared silently into the maze of passages. It got me thinking about how little we know about other people, their character, and their thoughts until something forces us to get to know them. I would have never, in a hundred years, thought Miss Wharburg to be the strong, empathetic person she had revealed herself to be. I promised myself that I would come back and see her when all this was over. But why was I fooling myself? This would never be over.

We reached a point in the tunnel where we saw the light coming from its end and stopped there.

"Someone ... should go on reconnaissance to take a peek and see what's going on at the school," said Jamie.

"I'll go," Tracy volunteered.

"No, not you," said Thomas, "I'll go. It's my fault we are in this hole, so I should take risks, not you."

"Have you forgotten who the chameleon is here?" Tracy insisted. "I have a better chance of observing without being seen, and that's why I am the one who needs to go. I don't mind your being chivalrous some other time, but please, not today. I think we will all agree that we've had enough of your initiatives for a while. I'm going, and I'll be careful, I promise."

"You'd better be," I said, speaking gravely to ensure that she understood the seriousness of the situation, "because if they catch you, they catch us all."

"Don't worry. I have no intention of letting them see me."

"Would you ..." I hesitated, "Would you agree to let me come with you, in your head? Just so you have another pair of eyes with you. I might help, you know?"

"Hmm, as long as you only observe and do no funny business with my body, I may consider letting you come along."

"Thanks, Tracy. I'll be good, I promise."

I was excited at the thought of being in Tracy's head, and not only to go scouting. I had gotten a glimpse of her inner soul before and found it irresistible. I know what you are about to ask: Was I out of my mind, thinking impure thoughts about Tracy at a time like this when our lives were in danger? Sure, but I've learned by now that life is short, and you must take what you can get when you can. Getting closer to Tracy was on my list of priorities, as long as it didn't hurt Jamie. And I had started to look at this "no hurting Jamie" business differently now. The way he had handled Schmidt—what we later started referring to as "the Bob incident"—didn't look like something a delicate boy would do. I found it hard to identify the angel of vengeance that Jamie had become with the sensitive, fragile boy he had shown me before. Or was I looking for ways to feel less obligated to him? I guess I was—I hate it when people dictate to me how to feel and behave. I hoped that killing Bob had brought closure to Jamie. And now I might be able to have a more—how should I say—uncomplicated relationship with Tracy.

She was getting ready to leave and hadn't answered me, so I joined my hands in mock prayer, and she laughed.

"Hop in, then," she said and opened her mind to me.

In a split second, I was in her head and was seeing through her eyes. I had to keep my eyes closed; seeing the same image from two different sets of eyes and angles is incredibly confusing. I could have reopened them once she got farther away from us, but keeping them closed helped my concentration. Besides, there was nothing much to see in that tunnel, so I kept them shut.

I used the minute or so until Tracy reached the end of the tunnel to settle in, and it was a unique experience. It's truly difficult to explain what it felt like. The best I can describe it is that I felt like I was lying on a floating bed of sugar-vanilla-scented feathers. It was cozy, warm, pleasant, and arousing,... but that was not what I meant to relate.

At the end of the tunnel, wooden stairs took us up to ground level. Tracy turned her head all around to make sure there was nobody close enough to see us, and then she started crawling toward the school. She moved very slowly and close to the ground. The shrubbery was high, so the only thing that might have given her away was the movement of the grass, but she moved very gingerly. Besides, the school was at least four hundred yards away, and we saw nobody looking in our direction. It's incredible how time flies; it had already been two hours since the first announcement, and as far as I could tell, the police were winding up their operation. From where we lay, we could see a segment of the road and watched a procession of police cars leaving. Five minutes later, silence returned to the school, and it looked like everybody, students included, had left. It might be a trap, but there was nothing more for us to see out there, so we crawled back to the tunnel.

Did you like what you saw? Tracy asked as we prepared to go inside again.

Sure did. They are gone.

That's not what I meant.

I knew what she meant. I had been prying in her mind a bit more than strictly needed for our mission.

Yes. I think you're beautiful inside and outside, I thought out loud.

You took some liberties with my thoughts and maybe saw things you weren't meant to see. We'll have to talk about this sometime, she said.

Yes, some time, I agreed. I was grateful that she was letting it go for now.

Back in the tunnel, I left Tracy's mind and searched for Barb's. She was in a conference room at what looked like a police station. That meant that the operation around the school had indeed ended, and we were not about to be ambushed when we came out of our hole. At first, I had no intention of reading Barb's mind—nothing in there interested me—but I sensed how furious she was and had to take a peek. What I saw explained it: she and Bob had been more to each other than mere colleagues and field operatives. I had to hand that to them both—they had never done or said anything to make me suspect that. So now we had a bitter enemy who surely was not less deadly than Bob—or rather, Schmidt—had been. Well, that couldn't be helped.

We climbed cautiously out of the tunnel, happy to breathe clean air again and to see the light of day. Jamie guided us to the barn where the SUVs were hidden, crossing fields and woods and avoiding the regular road. When we got there, Nolan was on edge, and the relief on his face when he saw us was enormous. He introduced Sandie perfunctorily to me, split us between the SUVs without wasting time, and got ready to move.

"I think Emily should be with us," I said, and Nolan simply nodded in assent.

"Everybody," he called out, "put your cellular phones in this basket. We can't take them with us because that's a sure way to get located."

A creek ran next to the barn, and Nolan put the basket onto a toy boat and then pushed it into the water. We watched it disappear downstream.

"Let them have fun chasing those," Nolan said with a smile. "Now, everybody, jump in! We'll drive keeping half a mile distance between us. No matter how fast or slow we go, you all have the motel's details of where we will meet. Remember that we are strangers to each other there. We will get rooms separately and keep our separate ways until I say so. Understood?"

Everybody nodded. We got into the SUVs. Ours was a black vehicle, and the other one was silver. Nolan led the way. He and Sandie didn't seem at all fazed that they had to leave what, until that day, had been a serene life. But then, that wasn't the first time they had had to do it, and maybe you get used to being a refugee after a while. I still had to adjust to it, but I'm adjustable. I have to be. Otherwise, I wouldn't be alive now.

I wanted to know a little about Sandie. After all, it is smart to know who you are running away from the law with.

"Tell me about Sandie," I asked Jamie.

Nolan was concentrating on driving, and I whispered to avoid distracting him. Jamie whispered back. We could have used telepathy, but talking when you're next to each other still feels more natural.

"There isn't much to tell. She's a great mother to Thomas—he has always been a little difficult. She needed a lot of patience when he was younger. She's divorced, and Thomas's father never kept in touch. What else do you want to know?"

"Is she level-headed? Can we trust her to keep her head if things get rough?"

"Oh, definitely. She's an ER nurse and as cool as they come. Once, when I was six, I fell in their garden and cut myself pretty badly. I was bleeding all over and scared to death. She came and cared for me, smiling as if it was nothing at all, and made me calm down in a minute. You'll be happy to have her with you if you are in trouble."

"Good," I said, "I needed to hear that."

CHAPTER 21

The trip was uneventful. I wondered why the feds hadn't put roadblocks all around Emendale, but maybe they were still chasing our phones down the creek. Be that as it may, we reached the motel marked on our map around dinnertime, and to say that I was famished is the understatement of the century. We got a room for Nolan and Jamie and another for Emily and me. The motel was on the outskirts of a big city—I can't tell you the city's name for reasons you will soon understand; it would place some people in danger, but take it from me that this was a big city.

The reception was in the main building, and the rooms were in a wing just outside. As soon as we got our keys and walked out, I grabbed Nolan's arm to get his attention.

"I'm hungry. What do you say that we ask for the whereabouts of the closest diner and go get some grub?" I asked, hopefully.

"Sorry, Tessa, no can do. You can get what you want from the dispensing machine in the lobby, and we still have some crackers and cheese in the SUV."

"Listen, Nolan, a healthy girl my age can't survive on crackers. I need food," I pleaded.

"I understand; I'm sorry, but we can't make ourselves conspicuous. I'll explain as soon as Sandie arrives and settles in."

Emily was standing nearby, apparently absorbed in thought. She had not spoken at all during the trip, and although none of us felt inclined to be chatty, I was worried about her state of mind. I dragged Nolan a little farther away and whispered to him, hoping she wouldn't hear.

"I worry that Emily is still in shock. What do you think?"

"I've no idea. She wasn't part of the original plan, and I don't know her, so I can't judge. Why don't you take her to your room and talk to her? Girls like to talk to girls, and perhaps she needs it."

"Okay, I'll do it, but there is another problem—neither Emily nor I have any clothes with us. Also, she smells a little and needs to take a shower right now if I have to be in the same room with her."

"That won't be a problem. Tracy loaded the SUV with clothes to the point there was no room for people to travel in. She only stopped when I threatened to unload everything and pick her clothes myself. Go and take a shower and use the motel's bathrobes. I'll send Tracy to you with two changes of clothes as soon as she gets here."

I thought that was a bright idea, and I took Emily's arm, nudging her to come. She came docilely. We climbed the stairs to our room on the second floor and locked the door behind us. I sat on the bed, planning to let Emily go first.

"Emily," I started to say, but I had to stop because she threw herself into my arms and started sobbing.

I'm not good at comforting people, not good at all. When tragedy strikes, I'm as useless as a broken coffeemaker, and I tend to run away and come back only when the floodgate of tears has closed again. But I had become sort of responsible for Emily, and this time I couldn't run away. I held her, saying stupid and useless things like "It's all right" and "It'll be okay" until the sobs stopped. Then I held her some more and slowly allowed her to move away from the embrace.

"I'm so scared," she sniffed.

"I know you are," I said, "but it'll be all right." There—stupid words again! But I didn't have any better ones.

"My mother must be worried sick."

"We'll find a way to let her know you're okay."

"Can't we call her now?"

"No, we are fugitives, remember? They'll find us if we call her and her phone is tapped."

I could have kicked myself for saying that because that opened the floodgate again, and she cried buckets for five more minutes. But eventually, the supply of tears gave out, and she blew her nose and looked at me.

"When ... when do you think we can return?" she asked.

"Back? To Emendale? We can't go back. If we do, we are dead. We will have to get your family to meet us somewhere else. You are an only child, right? Then your parents will certainly want to join you wherever you will be."

I wasn't so sure about that, but if I needed to lie to make Emily feel better, I was prepared to do it. As a rule, I never lie, except when necessary, and this was necessary. Besides, maybe making Emily's parents join her would be doable. I didn't know and was in no shape to think about it too much right then.

"So, what do we do now?"

"Baby, first of all, you take a shower 'cause you don't smell like violets. Then I'll take one too. I can't smell myself, but I'm sure I'm no Chanel Number Five, either. Then, by the time the others arrive and we have some clean clothes to put on, we'll scare up some food and see what's next. Right now, I don't know more about our immediate plans than you do."

A good shower can work miracles. I felt like a new girl after spending time under the jet. Even Emily looked slightly more encouraged, although she was still brooding and not inclined to chat. A knock on the door got me up from the bed that I was on, and a quick look through the peephole told me that the cavalry had arrived. Tracy was at the door with a duffel bag in her hand. I opened the door and dragged her in.

"You don't know how happy I am to see you," I said, and I had to hug her. "Traitor!" I yelled after sniffing her hair. "You showered before coming to bring me clothes," I mock complained. "Don't bother denying it; you smell good, I can tell."

Tracy laughed, and then she became serious.

"Hey, Emily," she said, speaking somberly, "how are you holding out?"

"I'll be okay," said Emily, but she didn't sound okay at all.

"Great. I've brought you a full change of clothes and some choices too. Take whatever you like," said Tracy and opened the duffel bag.

I let Emily choose first, and then I rummaged through the bag and picked the clothes I thought would be less flashy. I didn't know what we were about to do, but sure as hell, I wanted to look as low-key as possible. Emily and I got dressed, and I was pretty happy with the result. Tracy had style. When we were finally ready, Tracy stood up.

"Dad told me to call him and the others when you're ready. Your room is between mine and Dad's, so no neighbors will eavesdrop on us when he tells us what will happen next."

"I hope that whatever that is, it will be boring. I've had enough emotions for one day," I said.

"I don't know for sure, but I wouldn't count on that," said Tracy, and with a mischievous smile, she left to call the others.

CHAPTER 22

With six of us sitting on the bed, my room felt overcrowded. We sat in silence, waiting for Nolan to speak. He had dragged the only chair in the place near the bed, so we could hear him speak in a low voice. The feeling was almost like a military operation, with Nolan as the squad leader and us the troops. It brought back memories of the training camp where I had learned survival techniques and much more. Although I had bitched about all that training at the time, I was now mighty happy that I had learned a few tricks. I had a feeling that I was going to need them.

"So far, so good," said Nolan, maintaining an inscrutable expression. "You need to know that we haven't come to this particular place by chance or choice; Mark instructed us to come here."

"Did you speak to Mark?" Thomas asked, sounding almost incredulous.

"I did, and I do, but not directly. What I'm about to tell you is a well-kept secret. I wouldn't tell it to you if we were staying in Emendale, but there is no harm telling you now that we are on our way to meet Mark."

"We are?" Tracy asked open-eyed.

"Yes, honey. But let me explain this my way so I don't get confused. There is a place in this city, a foster home, which is my connection with Mark. When either he or I need to 'talk,' we call their number, and they act as intermediaries between us. I believe there are several intermediaries like it throughout the country, although I don't know for sure. That's how Mark keeps in touch with people like me without breaking cover."

"But how did you get in touch the first time?" I asked.

"I didn't; one of his men contacted me. I'll tell you the whole story when we have time, but now we don't. Anyway, when I was making the final preparations for our getaway from Emendale, Mark got word to me that he needed a favor. He wanted us to drive through here and pick up a boy, the foster son of his contacts in the city. His name is Robbie, and that's all I know—one of the good rules of Mark's organization is that you're never told more than you need to know. I have no idea why he has to come with us, but if Mark says so, that's how it is."

"How old is he?" Tracy asked.

"I don't know."

"Is he a telepath?" Thomas asked.

"I don't know that either. Tomorrow morning, I'll go by the house and pick him up, and then we'll leave. Meanwhile, I got some sandwiches and sodas from the lobby machine. Here," he added, handing over a large paper bag, "eat and then try to catch some sleep. Tomorrow we have another long travel day ahead of us."

We started guzzling our food—all of us except Emily. She got up from the bed and approached Nolan, who was at the door, about to leave, so I stopped chewing and joined them.

"I'm sorry," she said, and Nolan's expression turned from far away to attentive.

"Yes, Emily?" he said.

"What about me?"

"What do you mean?"

"I don't belong to your group. I got caught in … in all this by mistake."

"You belong now; you're one of us like everybody else," I hastened to say.

"Tessa's right," said Nolan.

He spoke softly and fatherly, and I admired him for it. I knew how tense he was and how much the responsibility for our safety weighed on his shoulders. I had read him a little, secretly. I had to do it because I needed to make sure that he was strong enough to lead us to safety.

"Thank you," she said, and a tear reappeared in her eyes. I thought she had consumed the entire supply, but apparently, it was endless.

"You don't need to thank me, you're my kid now, just like Tracy and Jamie."

"My parents must be so scared now—" she whispered and was about to go into crying mode again, so I had to intervene.

"Don't worry. We'll find a way to reassure them soon, right, Nolan?"

"Right," he said.

"Now get a bite to eat, and let me finish this sandwich that must have been made last year," I said, extracting a quick smile from her.

Soon everybody had eaten, and we said good night. Emily and I were again alone. I locked the door and turned off the light. Light from the lampposts outside still came in through the ineffective shades, but it was semi-dark enough to be able to sleep. The bed was okay, if not great, and the day's fatigue crashed on me as I slid under the sheets. I was ready to sleep, but Emily was still seated on the bed outside of the sheets.

"Come here," I ordered.

She nodded and came under the sheets on her side of the bed.

"Here, I said!"

I held out my arm in an inviting gesture. Emily hesitated for a moment, and then she got close. She put her head on my shoulder, and I hugged her closer. She shut her eyes and relaxed. I meant to reassure her, to make her feel part of the family, but the truth is that having her there with me made *me* feel good. It turns out that I am not entirely made of steel; I needed the reassuring warmth of another human being just as badly. The pleasant scent of her still-damp hair made me smile for some reason, and I tightened my hold on her for a moment.

"Good night," I whispered in her ear, and then I gave her a quick peck on the cheek.

"Night," she answered sleepily.

I don't know about her, but I was asleep two seconds later.

I get up fast when something intrudes on my sleep, and rapping on the window was what woke me up. I gazed at the clock on the nightstand next to me, which was the only useful thing in that room. The time was 2:15 AM. I squinted to sharpen my view and saw Jamie's unmistakable silhouette through the window, so I got up and slid the window open a little.

"What's the matter? It's the fuckin' middle of the night!" I hissed.

"I know, but I need to talk to you."

"Now? Can't it wait until morning?"

"No."

I gazed at Emily. She was fast asleep.

"Okay, talk," I whispered.

"Not through that slot. Come out here."

I wore flimsy shorts and a matching T-shirt, courtesy of Tracy, but the night wasn't cold, so I didn't need more. I took the room key and quietly closed the door behind me. Jamie motioned me to follow him, and we sat at the top of the stairs leading to our rooms. Now that I was wide awake, being out there rather than in that stuffy room was pleasant. Never mind that my head was light with the need to catch up with a lot more sleep.

"What's so urgent?" I asked.

"We haven't had a moment alone since this began, and since … what I did."

"You mean the Bob incident."

"Yes, if you want to call it that. I don't know what you think of me—"

"I think you're complex and surprising, and I haven't stopped liking you if that's what you're asking."

"It is, in a sense, but there is more. What I did, changed me. I feel free now, stronger, and I wanted you to know."

"You could have told me that over breakfast," I said, getting up, "but now that you've got it off your chest, we can go back to sleep."

Jamie grabbed my hand and pulled me down again.

"That's not it. Not all of it, I mean. Now I can see things clearly and know how I want it to be with us."

I knew what he meant, and that wasn't going the way *I* wanted.

"Jamie—you're sweet and dear to me, but there is no 'us,' you know that."

"But … I know that Anne's presence stood between us before, but no more, I swear. No more ghosts between us. She's gone."

"That's not Anne's fault. She was never a barrier between you and me. I told you who I am and the rule I live by, and we agreed not to make a big deal of this, remember?"

"I see. You said that you're unable to love, but I thought that maybe you didn't mean it. I still think you're behaving this way because you are afraid of commitment. I don't believe you don't love me; I can feel you do."

His shoulders were drooping, and the angst that his telemoticon broadcast was almost unbearable.

"You don't get me; it's quite the opposite. I do love you, but I'm not in love with you. That's because I love other people too, and I can't stop loving them because I love you. Can you understand that? Life is too short, and mine can end tomorrow morning or the day after. I can't afford to squelch my feelings for anybody because if I don't follow my heart today, they may be gone tomorrow."

As I spoke, Liv's image came before my eyes, and they got teary. I knew what I was talking about. *Damn!* I thought, *this tears thing is becoming a habit.*

Jamie nodded, pursing his lips a little.

"I see," he said.

"You see, but can you accept that this is who I am and that you can't own me?"

"It's hard, but I have no choice, right? I'll take what I can get."

"That's exactly what I do. I take what I can get from life when I can get it. And right now, you are a precious gift that life is giving me."

I stroked his arm gently, smiling encouragingly. I wanted to send him back to sleep, feeling good.

"I'll let you go back to sleep, then," he said and got up.

"Wait," I said, getting up too.

I put my arms on his shoulders and kissed him, first lightly and then more passionately. As I had already learned from our little picnic, he was a good kisser, and after a second, he responded as he knew how. That went on for a while until I pulled back.

"Now we can go back to sleep," I said.

An imperious knock on the door woke me up. The room clock showed the hour to be almost 10 AM, and I felt rested. At the door was Nolan, his expression dark and tense.

"What's up?" I asked, and before he could answer, the door opened again, and the others came in.

"Can't I have some privacy?" I complained. "This is not some kind of meeting room. I haven't brushed my teeth or washed my face yet, and you're not welcome to see me like this."

"Shut up, Tessa, this is serious."

As a rule, Nolan was soft-spoken, and this brusque response could only mean that more trouble was coming our way, so I obliged and shut my trap. The others waited in silence for Nolan to speak.

"I got up early because I wanted to leave as soon as possible. I went to pick up Robbie, but he wasn't there."

"So," Jamie asked, "where is he?"

"In custody. The police came half an hour before I arrived and arrested him. He's been brought in for questioning on a drug charge."

"So he's a drug dealer? Is that why he is in foster care?" I asked.

"That's a bullshit allegation. Robbie is no drug dealer. His foster father assured me. They made that up to be able to bring him in."

"This means that somehow, someone got wind that he is connected with Mark or that he is a telepath if he is one. Is he?" I asked.

"I don't know; I didn't think to ask."

"So what do we do now?" asked Thomas. "I think we need to leave immediately. We may be in danger too."

"I don't think so. If the police knew we are here, they would have come for us, not for Robbie," Sandie pointed out.

"That's a good point, Sandie," said Nolan.

"What do we know about Robbie?" I asked.

"We know where they took him, and I have his picture here,"

said Nolan. He showed us the portrait of a youth with brown eyes and a winning smile.

"He's cute," said Tracy.

"I say we go and get him out of there," I said. I was starting to have an idea. I get ideas, and often they get me into trouble. This one was a good candidate for trouble too.

"And how do we do that?" Jamie asked sarcastically. "Do we go to the police and ask pretty please?"

"Not quite, but almost. I haven't possessed anybody for quite some time now, and I think I miss it," I said with a wicked smile. "I will need someone to come with me and help me with a few things, but I think I can pull it off."

"I'll come with you," said Tracy without hesitation.

"Hey, hold your horses! I haven't given you permission to go anywhere, and surely not without me," said Nolan.

"You need to come too; someone has to drive and pick us up as we leave."

"You're out of your fucking mind!" Thomas spurted. "You'll get us all captured and killed."

"Thomas has a point, too, Tessa," said Nolan. "If we come out in the open, they will know that we're here, which will put everybody in danger."

"They don't have to understand that right away. And what is the alternative? Does it feel right to you to abandon Robbie here without trying to get him out? He appears to be important to Mark."

Nolan was silent for a few seconds while he scanned the room and the faces in it.

"Let's hear your plan," he said at last.

CHAPTER 23

Nolan had parked the SUV in an alley behind the police station building. Tracy and I sat in silence while I got myself ready. We had checked out of the motel, and everybody else had left in Sandie's SUV, heading to the next meeting point. The three of us would be joining them after we got Robbie out. If we didn't get caught, that is.

I took Robbie's portrait and gazed at it intently, and then I opened my mind for a short-range scanning. I hoped that they hadn't taken him to an underground cell or someplace where I might not be able to reach him. I also hoped that he would not offer resistance if he noticed that someone was trying to read him. There were too many unknowns and too many ways in which this might go wrong. Tracy and I had come up with three different plans. Which one we would use depended on the topography of the place and the number of people around. I hoped that we hadn't forgotten to consider something of critical importance.

I closed my eyes and breathed deeply, and bingo! I was in Robbie's head. He had offered no resistance, not even for a second, so I guessed he wasn't a telepath.

"I'm in," I said.

I opened my eyes for a second and saw the relief on Nolan's and Tracy's faces. I closed them again and concentrated on Robbie. I was sitting in a room, bare but for a metal table and facing chairs. In the chair facing Robbie sat a plainclothes policeman. The room had a high window with bars on it, and from what I could see, it meant that the room was on the ground floor level. That was a bonus since it meant that we wouldn't have to pass through different floors or ride in elevators and run into too many people on our way out.

Now, this was the tricky part. When communicating with someone you don't know for the first time, you will likely spook him. I didn't know how Robbie would react, but it might ruin everything if he got severely spooked. I had no other way to do it, though.

Robbie, I'm here to help. Mark sent us. Please listen and say nothing. If you hear me, touch your nose with your finger.

When Robbie did as asked, a heavy weight lifted off my mind.

"He's listening," I said quickly in the SUV. I didn't want to keep Nolan and Tracy hanging.

Great! Listen, Robbie, we will get you out of here, okay? It will be tricky and may take a while, so please play along. Don't do anything rash and take no initiative, okay? If you understand, touch your nose again.

Robbie touched his nose again, and I concentrated on the man seated before him, who was now speaking.

"Did you think about what I said to you before? Are you ready to cooperate? The federal agent will be here in an hour, and if you are willing to cooperate, you'll be home by dinnertime."

"Tell me again, what do you want from me?"

Good boy! I thought and wasn't sure if I had pushed that thought to him too. He was getting me information. I was impressed by the calm way that he was taking all this.

"We know you have contacts with a dangerous group of criminals who are self-professed mind-readers. You were seen talking to one of them last night, one we were keeping surveillance on, but he got away, and we lost him. We need to know who else he is in touch with and where he's hiding. You give him to us, and you go free."

Bullshit! Robbie thought, but his expression remained relaxed.

"I don't know what you're talking about," he said softly.

"If that's how you want to play it," said the cop, "there is nothing more to say. The feds will deal with you, and I don't envy you. I could have helped you if you decided to come clean before they got here, but since you haven't, they'll get it from you one way or another."

The cop got up and was about to leave, so it was then or never.

Robbie, don't freak out. I'm going to get into this cop's head, and when I do, I'll be in control. Whatever he says after that, it's me saying it, and it's true.

Head-hopping is an art that I perfected when saving Mary, my boss, in Switzerland. At the time, I had had to jump from the head of one ugly goon to another under much more difficult conditions than what I had now. Crashing the party in this cop's brain and taking control of it was a piece of cake in comparison, and I did it in a second. I had no time for niceties, so taking over this time was a bit brutal, but I couldn't afford to do it gradually. Once I was in, I smiled a big smile and spoke.

"That's me, Tessa. Nice to meet you, Robbie."

I didn't have the time to be too explorative, but I couldn't help noticing how good he looked. He was more or less my age, very well built, dark-skinned, with a winning smile and deep brown eyes. Twitching biceps too, and I guessed that his abs had to match them. But there was no time for those kinds of thoughts. I filed them away for later reference and concentrated on the job at hand.

"Nice to meet you too, Tessa. That's a neat trick you do. So what's next?"

"Now we get you out of here," I said. "Do you know the topography of the building?"

"Yes, as we leave this room and turn right, there is a short corridor that ends in a ninety-degree bend, which opens into the reception area. There is a desk there, with the sergeant on duty, watching the entrance, and beyond that are other offices."

"Okay, we'll stop at the corner. When it's time, you run out through the main door as fast as you can. A girl will be waiting for you outside. Her name is Tracy, and she will take you to our getaway vehicle. Got that?"

"Yes. When you walk with me, grab my arm. That's how this cop walked me before, and if anybody sees us, they'll think everything's normal."

I opened the door using the electronic key hanging from the cop's belt, and we walked to the end of the corridor. I peeked around the corner. The desk was right before the glass doors that led outside; the cop at the desk was doing paperwork. It was lunchtime, and the building was quiet, so those were the best conditions we could have hoped for.

"I'll go now. As soon as you see me on the floor keeping that cop busy, run for the door and don't look back, okay?"

"Got it," Robbie said.

I opened my eyes in the SUV for a split second—I didn't want to risk losing control of the cop's body. "Plan A, Tracy," I said, and then I concentrated again on my host.

"Good luck," I said to Robbie and came out into the open.

The cop at the door gazed at me, and right then, a uniformed one came out of one of the offices.

"How's it going, Spencer?" the sergeant on duty threw at me without any real show of interest. "You done with the package you prepared for the feds?"

"Yeah," I said, "I came out for some fresh air. I'm not feeling too good. Must've eaten something bad."

"I told you that if you keep going to that Chinese place, you'll catch something. They cook bats and dogs," said the sergeant with a little laugh.

I walked past the desk and a few paces to the left of the entrance, and then I let myself drop to the floor. The sergeant jumped up, crying, "Spencer!" and he and the uniformed cop ran to me. I thought more dramatic effects would help, so I made the body shake, like someone having an epileptic seizure. The two cops were all over me, and I had to keep it going until I was sure that Robbie was far away.

Faking a seizure in a body you are controlling is hard work. It demanded all my attention, but I felt that the SUV was moving, and then I allowed the cop's body to stop shaking and let it lie there, breathing normally. The other two cops were standing helplessly by their colleague's body, and a few others had come running out of their offices and joined them. That's when an ambulance pulled up next to the door, and two medics came in carrying a stretcher. They checked the cop's vital signs, put him on the stretcher, and took him to the ambulance that drove away with a wailing siren. The time had come to say goodbye to him. I felt sorry for him; by the time he managed to explain to himself what had happened, he would have to deal with the fact that the prisoner left in his care had escaped.

"Good to be back," I said after I let go of the poor cop.

Robbie and Tracy were gazing at me.

"Awesome, Tessa!" said Tracy.

"You were fantastic," said Nolan, without taking his eyes off the road.

"I don't know how to thank you," said Robbie.

"Don't thank me yet. We're not out of the woods," I pointed out.

"You're much cuter than when you were inside that cop," said Robbie.

I acknowledged the compliment with a cute smile—at least, I hoped it was cute—cocking my head to one side. I'm afraid I might have blushed a little.

I thought I saw a twitch of disapproval on Tracy's lips, but I might have been wrong.

CHAPTER 24

"Listen," said Nolan.

He had turned on the police frequency scanner, and excited voices were coming through it. There were so many who spoke unclearly that I couldn't understand a thing.

"What are they saying?" I asked.

"They are setting up roadblocks at various locations, looking for Robbie. They refer to him as 'the fugitive,' but it's clear who they are talking about."

"So, what do we do?"

"We get off the highway. I had expected something like this to happen, and I have identified a good place to go until things cool off. Meanwhile, Tessa, you check out with Jamie where they are. They must have already gotten beyond the state line and the roadblocks, so they shouldn't be in danger, but they need to know that we are stuck here for a while."

"I'm on to it right away," I said.

Jamie, I called.

Reaching out to him was easy for me by then. When communicating is the challenge, it's all a matter of how close you two are.

The closer you are, the faster and easier it is to initiate a connection.

Tessa! I was worried sick. Where are you?

We are okay. We got Robbie as planned, but we won't be able to join you yet. The police are setting up roadblocks to try to find him, and we need to lie low for a day or two until they give up.

But that means that you may miss the plane.

What plane?

Ask my father; he'll explain.

All right. I'll talk to you soon.

Tessa ...

Yes?

I—

Don't say it, dammit! Don't think it. Not while we are on the run, please.

I broke contact before things got too awkward.

"I told Jamie. What plane is it that we are going to miss?"

"Sandie's big mouth!" said Nolan. "All right, this is the thing. We need to be at a certain small airfield in a little more than two days. A plane is scheduled to pick us up from there and take us to Mark. That's why we had to wait before leaving Emendale while Mark was organizing it. The plane will land and take off immediately. It cannot wait for anybody. The flight is not registered anywhere, and it has a tiny window of opportunity to make the trip without being discovered. It masquerades as a legitimate flight. The trip from here to that airfield will take a little more than eight hours, so we still have time to get there and catch our flight."

"If we can get through," I observed.

"If," Nolan concurred.

"A campground. Are you serious?" I asked.

Nolan had taken us through bumpy roads into a wooded area. The road led to an entrance with a sign saying, "Pinewood Flat Campground – Welcome!" A camper trailer was parked in the shade of the trees, but the place was otherwise empty. We stopped our SUV at a distance from that camper trailer to make a statement that we were not there to socialize, and Nolan cut the engine.

"This is hopefully the last place where the police will look for us, so we can hide here for a day and see what develops. Luckily, we bought enough food when we stopped for gas. I have a tent that will turn our SUV into a cozy place to sleep. Robbie, come here and give me a hand to set it up."

"I'll look around a bit while you do it," I said. I needed to stretch my legs and my brain as well. "Are you coming with me, Tracy?"

"Sure," she said and jumped down after me.

The place was beautiful, and I might have enjoyed it if I wasn't busy thinking about how to avoid getting murdered by a bunch of vicious killers. We strolled down a path that took us to a stream that cooled the air all around. We sat on the bank of the stream, and I let my feet dangle in the cold water.

"Weird, right?" said Tracy.

"What?"

"This. So peaceful and beautiful, but so not real for us."

"I see what you mean. We don't have the freedom to think and act like regular teenagers. But then, I never was one."

"I was, once. I haven't given it up yet. And by the way, Robbie is yummy."

"You can have him," I said. Somehow, it looked to me like Tracy was asking for permission or something.

"I've seen how he looks at you," she objected.

"That's because I saved him."

"Yeah, sure. That's not the vibe, though."

"Listen, things are complicated enough as it is. I don't need them to become messier."

"Complicated how?"

"With Jamie ... and you," I said, and I don't know why my voice came out so thin in the end.

Tracy took a long look at me, then got closer and kissed me on the corner of my mouth. Then, she hugged me and held me close.

"I agree. Let's not make things more complicated than they are. If we are alive in a couple of days, everything will be all right, and we will be free to plan how to mess our lives up," she joked.

But I was in no mood for joking.

"Some things will never be the same or all right again," I said. I had been suddenly reminded of Liv. "Let's make the most of it while we can."

I returned her hug, got up, took her hand, and pulled her after me. We walked back in silence.

Nolan had prepared a decent dinner with the groceries we had bought at the gas station. We ate early because we had skipped lunch and made do with some cinnamon bars on the road. He also produced a folding table and chairs out of nowhere; we had disposable plates, forks, and knives. It felt like we were seated at a real dinner table. The atmosphere wasn't exactly that of a high-school campfire, but it was as merry as it could be. After the food was gone, Tracy decided it was time to ask some questions.

"So, who are you, Robbie?" she asked.

"I'm Robbie."

"Very funny. Throw us a bone! Where are you from? How did

you end up in that foster home? Are you a telepath? Give us the goods!"

"Look, Tracy, I know I owe you a lot, and I don't want you to think I'm not grateful because I am. Immensely. But I don't think that we should talk about me right now. We may still get caught, and the less information we have about each other, the better. I'll tell you everything once we are safe."

"Oh, all right. You and your secrets! I'm going to take a walk before going to bed. The least you can do is come with me and keep me safe from wild animals."

"Sure, I'll fend the bears off," said Robbie with a broad smile.

"There are no bears in this area," said Nolan, "but don't get too far away all the same. As to sleeping arrangements, the girls can sleep in the tent, which has a soft mattress, and Robbie and I will sleep in the car."

"I'm turning in," I said. "Good night."

I had something to do before I could even consider sleeping, and I had to be alone to do it.

CHAPTER 25

I n the tent, I had the privacy I needed to handle what I had to do. I had to get to the bottom of what was happening with Liv. I had put that off for too long, but in all fairness, I wasn't neglecting her; I had been busy staying alive. I lay down on the mattress, which was the softest thing I had lain on lately, and I closed my eyes. In a flash, I saw through Liv's eyes. She was at home—our home—seated at her desk. Her calendar was open before her, and she was staring at it. It was a handsome, leather-covered appointment book that I had bought her as a present. She turned a page to tomorrow's date, and her eyes went to the only entry that said, "Interview, 9:30." What was she interviewing for? Was she going to leave Mary's unit? Something was going on, and I needed to find out what it was.

Liv and I had our way of starting a remote conversation. I would take control of her right hand and gently stroke her cheek. I hesitated for a moment, and then I did so.

Tessa? Is that you? You can't be here. Go away! Go away and don't come back! If you don't go away, I'll wear a shield from now on. Leave me alone, please, and never come back!

The rejection in her thoughts hit me hard. I was hurt as I had

140

never been hurt before. I made her make a fist with her hand, then waved it before her eyes and broke contact. She appeared to have chosen her loyalty to the service over me, so if that were what she wanted, I'd let her go. But not before I knew what she was interviewing for.

Sleeping with the sounds of nature, like those you hear in the woods, is soothing. Although it counts as "natural," what woke me up in the middle of the night was an unmistakable and distinct noise coming from the other corner of the tent, where Tracy was sleeping, or rather not sleeping.

I never intrude on other people's privacy, so I didn't tell her to keep it quiet. After all, she was entitled to have some fun with Robbie. I had seen how hard she had worked for it.

I have this natural clock that wakes me up precisely one minute before the alarm goes off. If I don't have an alarm clock, it still wakes me up right on time, as long as I make myself believe that I am setting up the alarm before going to sleep. I'm told that it's not something special and that many people without any telepathic ability can do that. Anyway, it comes in very handy for me, and that evening I had "set up" the alarm to wake up in time to go to Liv's interview with her. I know you'll say I was being insanely possessive and that if Liv didn't want to have anything more to do with me, I had to leave her alone. But I loved her, and she had loved me, and before I could let her go, I had to know why she had changed.

The smell of coffee made me jump out of bed. I ran to the water faucet to brush my teeth. I must do that when I wake up, or my whole day is ruined. I can't understand people who wake up and drink coffee without brushing their teeth first. Or, God forbid, couples who kiss in bed when they wake up. Gross!

I returned from the water fountain to the coffee poured into Styrofoam cups on our table. Tracy and Robbie were drinking already, and Nolan was fiddling with something that was meant to look like breakfast. I gazed at Tracy, and she blushed. She knew that I knew, and I think the butterflies and the birds couldn't help knowing it, too; she was so radiant.

"Good morning," said Nolan. "I have been listening to the police radio. It's too soon to tell for sure, but it sounds like they may be giving up and folding their roadblocks. There are talks on the radio about the fugitive having crossed the state line. I'll keep listening, and if everything looks good, we may leave by noon."

"That's great news," I said. "I wanted to ask you guys to forgive me for not keeping you company. I need to be on my own for one hour or so. If you don't mind, I'll stay in the tent, and I'll ask you not to come in there until I'm done."

"What's the matter, Tessa?" Nolan asked. He looked concerned.

"Nothing, private stuff. I need to check on someone and make sure that she's okay. Do you mind?"

"No, no, sure. Go ahead."

I had half an hour before Liv's interview, so I finished my coffee and went into the tent, followed by Tracy's and Robbie's gaze. Who knows what they were thinking. Probably that my less-than-joyful mood had to do with them—people are so self-centered. In the tent, I lay down and closed my eyes. It was lucky that Liv had no way of knowing that I was spying on her. When we lived together, she had permitted me to read her whenever I wanted, but I always told her after I did. This time, she wouldn't know, which bothered me for some reason.

I caught up with her as she was leaving the apartment, dressed in her formal navy uniform, in which she was so sexy. Seeing her walk through the familiar places gave me a pang of nostalgia. She walked toward the ESA Unit's office building, and I took some comfort in enjoying the clear morning air and the familiar surroundings. When she reached Mary's office, her secretary greeted her with a broad smile.

"Welcome, Lieutenant Hellman; please walk right in. You are expected," she said.

Liv opened the door of Mary's office and walked in but stopped in her track because it was not Mary in the room but a stout, bald man.

"I'm sorry," she said, "there must be a mistake. I'm here to see Miss Mary Payne."

"No mistake, Lieutenant; please come in and take a seat."

"I don't understand. I was told that I had an appointment with Miss Payne, and this is her office, or am I in the wrong place?"

"Miss Payne is no longer heading this unit; she has been reassigned. As of today, I am running it. My name is Wickgram, no first name. Please sit down. It's the second time I've asked you."

Liv gazed at him intently. His eyes were cold, and his manners offensively polite. She found him repulsive; I could tell—I was in her head and feeling what she felt. But she was a soldier trained to obey, so she sat down.

"That's better. Now let me tell you why you are here. Your knowledge of the physiology of telepathic activity is valuable to us, but no less so is your knowledge of one agent who has gone rogue. I'm sure you know who I'm talking about."

"Tessa."

"Right, Tessa. She has taken part in the murder of one of our most valued operatives, and then she has disappeared. We are looking for her everywhere. As you know, she can be extremely dangerous."

"I can't believe that she killed anybody but in self-defense. I know her."

"But you also know that her brain is unstable because she was exposed to radiation that changed her brain patterns. The latest test results clearly show that; you have seen that yourself. The Tessa you knew is not the person she is today, and tomorrow she may become a serial killer. She must be stopped."

You mean the test results that you or your minions falsified to mislead Tessa and me so she would limit the use of her power, you fat pig! If you think I'm going to help you, you're a bigger fool than you look, Liv thought, and it warmed my heart. It also explained why she had told me to use telepathy only when really needed. It was a way of blinding me a little that the agency had come up with. *It's lucky that the Director warned me that I should break contact with Tessa until she was safe,* Liv added to herself.

It was also lucky that the Director—meaning ESA15—was not near me, or I would have kissed him, and he would have hated it.

"What do you want me to do?" Liv asked.

"We know that Tessa trusts you, that you are ... friends, so to speak. We want you to bring her in so we can cure her without damaging her. She's too precious an operative for us to give up on her. Otherwise, if our field operatives find her, I'm afraid they'll have to kill her. The order, right now, is to shoot on sight."

I know what kind of "cure" you plan for her, the permanent one with a bullet in her head.

I knew that Liv was intelligent, but seeing that she wasn't buying any of that bullshit was heartwarming.

"I'll do what I can," she said, "but you need to know that since she left for her mission, Tessa has not been in touch with me. I don't know where she is or what her plans are. If Tessa contacts me, I'll do my best to convince her to turn herself in and get the help she needs. I don't know if she'll contact me ever again, just as

I don't know why she hasn't been in contact until now. If I hear from her, I'll report to you immediately."

"I expect nothing less from you, Lieutenant; thank you. I am counting on you. You can take the rest of the week off while we reorganize this unit."

"Thank you, sir," said Liv.

She got up and left in a hurry. Outside, she walked until she reached a bench by the park, then she sat on it and cried silently. I ached to comfort her, but I knew that I shouldn't.

CHAPTER 26

I broke contact with Liv, and then I did a little crying of my own. Sometimes it helps, and I'm not against it as long as nobody sees me doing it. This time, it relieved a little of my pressure. I dried my eyes, forced a smile on my lips, and got out of the tent. Nolan and Tracy were leaning on the SUV, and as they saw me, Tracy took a step toward me. Her brow was furrowed, and she looked troubled.

"What's going on?" I asked.

"Emily is missing," she said.

"What do you mean, 'missing'?"

"Jamie just told me. They got up this morning, and they went to her room when she didn't show up for breakfast. Her bed hadn't been slept in."

"Damn it! How could they leave her alone?"

"They didn't think it was a problem."

"Oh, shit! If the feds catch her, she'll bring them to Sandie."

"Don't worry," said Nolan. "They have already left and are heading for the next meeting point. Emily doesn't know where that is. Anyway, it's bad."

"Bad? It's awful! Emily is confused, and who knows what she'll do. I need to get to her," I said.

"Do you think you can?"

"I'm sure I can," I said.

"Then you'd better do it while we drive. The road is open. The police have removed all the roadblocks, and we need to get going now. We are in danger of missing the plane as it is."

Robbie came from the woods, where I guess he had gone to relieve himself. Nolan urged him to give him a hand to fold the tent. We all helped pack, and ten minutes later, everything had been loaded in the SUV, and we started moving. I closed my eyes and searched for Emily. I didn't know her approximate whereabouts, which made it more difficult than usual to make contact. I made a few false connections, but eventually, I found her and read her confused and anguished mind.

"Oh, my God, she's going back to Emendale!" I cried.

"How could she be so stupid?" Tracy said, speaking angrily.

"She couldn't bear the separation. She called her mother. The feds had come to see her, and she convinced Emily to come back and that she'll be safe."

"You must stop her," Nolan said.

"There is nothing I can do; she'll get there in less than a half-hour."

"Talk to her, take control of her body, whatever it takes," said Tracy.

"I don't know this girl, but she sounds nuts to me," said Robbie. "Perhaps you should leave her alone. Whatever trouble she's in, she has brought it on herself."

That simply enraged me.

"You're right; you don't know her, so stay out of this," I said, and I didn't try to sound polite. "Now, all of you, shut up and let me work."

I got back to Emily, seeing through her eyes. She was on a bus heading into Emendale. God knew how she had gotten that far without much money, probably hitchhiking.

Emily, get off that bus, I pushed a thought to her. She didn't react, and I didn't know if she had heard me, but at that moment, I realized that it no longer mattered. A police roadblock appeared a hundred yards ahead of the bus, which stopped with screeching brake sounds. The driver opened the door and stepped down to talk to the officers. I did the only thing that occurred to me—I took possession of Emily's body and made her jump down, slide along the bus's length, and run for the woods. I hoped that she would have a chance if she could get away unseen. And for a moment, I thought she did, but then shouts of "Stop! Hands up!" told me that the feds had seen her. It was too late to get away, so I made her stand and put her hands on her head, and then I let go of her body. A figure approached, and I saw that it was Barb. She wore a tense expression as she stood a few paces from Emily. Without provocation, she shouted again, "Stop, or I'll shoot!" Then she shot Emily point-blank.

I felt the bullet tear through Emily's body and heard the scream of horror in her mind. I fell backward in my seat, too horrified to speak.

"What happened, Tessa? What happened?" I heard Tracy's voice as if it were coming from afar.

But I couldn't speak or breathe. All I could do was double up and cry.

It took a lot of holding and talking to me on Tracy's part to calm me down, but eventually, I did, at least in part. I was still under the impression of that bullet. I had "died" before, but the first time was with someone I didn't care about; this time, I cared deeply for her and felt responsible.

"She could be alive if I had let her stay on that bus. Barb wouldn't have killed her with witnesses around," I murmured.

"Don't beat yourself up," said Nolan, "she would have killed her anyway, there or elsewhere. Once she decided to go back to Emendale, she was doomed. You did what you could to save her. It's not your fault."

"Thank you, Nolan. I know you're right, but I feel awful all the same. I promised to protect her and told her everything would be all right, but it wasn't."

It was night outside, and we were driving slowly on a narrow road. Tracy was still holding me, and I was grateful for that; I needed to feel her close.

"There are some promises made in good faith that it turns out you can't keep," said Nolan, "but here's one I'm keeping. This is the airfield, and we made it on time. There's Sandie."

I looked out and saw the silver SUV parked near a fence. Jamie and Thomas came running to us. We all got out of the SUVs and hugged, laughing.

"Save the celebrations for later," said Nolan. "We have ten minutes before the airplane arrives. We must turn the field lights on exactly two minutes before the hour. The light switch is here." Nolan opened a cabinet door next to the runway entrance and exposed an electric board with a big lever at the center. "Get ready," he ordered.

Precisely two minutes before the hour, Nolan turned the lights on, and we heard the noise of an approaching jet aircraft. It landed on the hour, and we ran to it as soon as it stopped on the runway and turned around, ready to take off again. It was a small jet aircraft, seating twelve. The front door opened, letting stairs drop down, and the pilot's head popped out of the door.

"Quick!" said the pilot. "We are leaving in two minutes."

He didn't need to spur us; we wanted to be on that plane badly enough. We ran up the stairs and took seats at random.

"Don't all of you sit on the same side; we need balance. Spread out on both sides," the pilot ordered. He pulled up the stairs, closed the door, sat in his seat, and the plane started to roll. One minute later, we were airborne, and I felt like breathing again. I had no idea where we were going, but as it was, I didn't care.

CHAPTER 27

The flight took us about four hours, and it was still dark when we landed. I can't tell you exactly where we landed, that's a big secret, but I can say that it is a small island in the Caribbean Sea. You don't need to know more than that.

I had managed to sleep a little during the flight, but I didn't feel rested at all; like the others, I was still wasted from the tension of the last few days. The pilot said a perfunctory goodbye and seemed happy to get rid of us. On our part, we thanked him warmly on the way out, but all we got in return was a blank stare. A big car was waiting for us. The driver wasn't chatty either and spoke only with Nolan. A drive of about twenty minutes took us to a place that looked like a holiday resort. A cheerful woman—cheerful despite the ungodly hour, which I thought was impressive—gave us keys and showed us to our rooms.

"You will find everything you need in your room," she said when she opened the door of mine.

"If it has a bed, that's all I need for now," I said, and she smiled understandingly before silently shuffling out of the room. She walked almost as if she had wheels in her soles.

There was a bottle of water on a nightstand next to the bed, from which I drank a little before crashing on the mattress without bothering to undress.

I opened my eyes, sensing that something wasn't right, and of course, it wasn't. There was a man in my room, looking down at me. I jumped to my feet, ready to deal with any danger he might present, but then I remembered where I was and how I had got there, and simply waited for him to speak.

"Good morning, Tessa," said the man.

I studied him for a few seconds. He was about forty-five years old, with butterscotch hair and blue eyes. He was slim and smartly dressed in what looked like golf attire.

"Who are you?" I asked.

"I'm your host. Why don't you go to freshen up, and then we can speak?"

"Does speaking involve eggs and coffee?" I asked.

He smiled a pleasant smile. "Of course, we don't want you to starve," he said.

"Then, give me ten minutes to shower, and I'll be with you."

"No problem. You'll find suitable clothes in that closet over there," he said.

The closet was filled with a broad variety of clothes, not exactly my size but close enough. I'm not a slave to fashion, so I grabbed the first change of clothes I felt would be okay for me. I walked into the bathroom, locked the door safely after me, and did my morning routine, which I concluded with a quick jump in and out of the shower. After that, I felt much better and dressed up in clothes that were surprisingly soft to the touch. The man was waiting for me exactly where I had left him.

"After you," I said, and he led the way.

The man—Jacob, it turns out was his name—led me to a veranda with a fantastic view of the seashore. Five small, round tables were waiting for customers, but we were alone. We barely managed to sit at the table before a waiter came along and took our orders. I was too hungry to waste time asking questions, so I shot mine at him. Jacob ordered coffee.

"So what is this, a resort for high-level executives?"

"Actually, yes, although that's only our façade. Nobody can get in unless he's invited."

"I assumed so. This is not the first place I've seen, which is not what it seems. So what does the façade hide?"

"It hides Mark's operation—one of Mark's operations."

"If I need to get details from you one by one, bits and pieces, let me know. I'm a bit too tired for this."

"No, of course. I'll tell you what you need. I thought that I would answer your questions first. I don't want to overwhelm you."

"I see. You can start by telling me who Mark is. Or maybe that's you?"

"No, of course, my name is Jacob." He gave out a little laugh and then asked, "You didn't think that Mark was a person, did you?"

"Does that make me look stupid? Because I did. So, if he's not a person, what is he, a Martian?"

"It's not a 'he,' it's an 'it.' Mark is short for Mission Ark. The name is a play on Noah's Ark, the one that saved the species that repopulated the Earth after the flood."

"So, which species are you going to save? And when is the flood due?"

"Mostly telepaths, but also a few other people with different special abilities. And our flood has been brewing for quite some time. A few governments have set up secret agencies that should deal with 'the problem,' the problem being you, for instance, and others like you. Essentially, those are well-organized murder squads."

My response was delayed because my mouth was full of eggs and toast. They had mercifully been dished out to me quickly. I had to swallow a little before I was able to speak again.

"A few governments? Shit! I thought that we were dealing only with a bunch of fanatics in our government, but now you're telling me that this is an international effort?"

"Well, not international. Only a few countries, but that's challenging enough."

"So, who set up this Mark thing?"

"As you know better than me, telepathy doesn't necessarily run in the family—it may, but most often, it doesn't. Some powerful men have gifted children, although they themselves have no special abilities. A few of them have had a child killed by one of these task forces. As I said, they are potent men because some have positions in government agencies, and others are wealthy. So they got together and created Mission Ark. This is an important center for the mission. Here we take in people who had to run away, give them a new identity, and allow them to live their lives under a different name in a different place. We employ a few masters at document and official records' forging, and we have been very successful so far."

"Mm, it looks to me that you are playing with fire. This game is not for amateurs. Some people you have sent back under an assumed name may get caught, and then the bad guys will know about you and get to you."

"We are not dilettantes, you know? Some of us come from sophisticated agencies. So now tell me, do you know where we are?"

"No, but I'm sure to find out soon."

"No, you aren't. You won't find any information anywhere on this base from which you'll be able to know where we are. You may try to guess, but I assure you that you'll come up with the wrong answer. We took precautions."

"Good for you. So are you planning to send us back soon?"

"We are planning to send your friends back soon, not you."

"What?"

"You are too important. We would like you to work with us as part of the team."

I seldom am left speechless, but that was one occasion when I didn't know what to say. Regardless of how beautiful it was, I didn't want to be stuck on that island for the rest of my life. On the other hand, I also didn't want to go back into hiding in some godforsaken place under a stupid name like Margarita or something. So I did what I always do; I stalled.

"I'll consider it after I know more about you and what you want me to do here."

"Fair enough."

"When do I meet other people who work here?"

"After you say 'Yes.' Until then, I'm the only one you see. We never expose our guests to more than one operative."

"Fair enough," I had to say.

CHAPTER 28

Jacob took me to an underground room that had clear signs of being a command post. Large screens covered two of its walls, and more computers than I ever had seen in one place were distributed around on long tables. The explanation he gave me was long and detailed, and at times it made my head spin. From that room, they followed countless subjects they had relocated and organized into cells. Other equipment helped predict those cells' danger factors to alert them in time. Another screen followed the known enemy task forces and their activities, displaying alerts and other information.

"We must end our tour as quickly as we can," said Jacob at the end of the elaborate explanation. "This is our command post, and it is staffed twenty-four-seven by three to six people. I have cleared the room to show it to you, but I can't keep it idle for long."

I took a deep breath before speaking. I knew I would disappoint him, and I wasn't looking forward to it because I also knew that I very likely owed my life to him.

"Look, Jacob, I appreciate your showing me all this. Your operation is very impressive, but I am not someone you can put underground in a room with no windows and ask to gaze at a screen all day. I truly stink at this kind of work."

"We know you better than you can imagine, and we understand that."

"How can you? I only got here ..."

"Oh, we do; it doesn't matter how; you'll know what we do in due course. What matters now is that we are not planning to ask you to work here. But look at this screen. Do you see this orange dot here on the map? According to our software's prediction, that marks a place where some telepaths will be found in the next month or so. They are likely to get killed unless we do something about it. And to do something about it, we need boots on the ground, an agent with special abilities like yours who can help change the course of events. That's what we want to offer you."

"I'm in!" I yelled.

I know I'm impulsive; no need to rub it in! I had spent the past thirty minutes worrying that I would spend the rest of my days in a stuffy basement, goggling at computer screens. Now I felt that I was being saved, and my reaction was instinctive.

"I'm glad, but are you sure? You didn't have the time to consider the risks. The job I'm offering you is dangerous. You don't have to take it. Instead, you may be relocated like your friends, if you want. I want to make sure that you understand that we never force anybody into a dangerous situation."

"I'm fast at considering and, yes, I'm in. A hundred percent!"

"Welcome, then. Just as I promised you dangers, I can promise you that we will always watch your back and do what we can to get you out. You can ask Robbie."

"Robbie is an agent?"

"He certainly is, and you will be working with him occasionally."

"But he has no special abilities. He's not a telepath, I'm sure."

"You're right. Robbie is not a telepath, but as far as special abilities are concerned, he definitely has one."

"Which is what?"

"I don't want to spoil the surprise for you. Ask him to show you."

"I hope it's a good one that I can use to get me out of trouble sometime; he owes me big time."

I don't like mysteries, so I went to look for Robbie. He was taking a nap at the beach when I found him.

"You owe me an explanation," I said.

"About what?"

"You didn't want to tell me anything about you or your special ability, if you have one, while we were running away from the feds. Now you're out of excuses, so let's have it."

He had a cat's smile on his face, from which I assumed that he was going to enjoy telling me.

"I wondered when you would get around to asking me. Fine. Do you see the beer bottle I'm keeping in the icebox? Keep watching it."

As I watched it, the bottle simply lifted itself out of the icebox slowly and elegantly. It flew my way and stopped right in midair before me.

"Cool," I said.

"You can grab it now," Robbie said.

I did, and then I decided to test Robbie's power.

"I'm holding it; try to take it away from me," I said.

I felt a little pull coming from the bottle I held in my hand, but it had no kick. Robbie's furrowed brow told the story.

"I can't," he said.

"I see. It's a nice parlor trick, kind of a Friday night psychokinesis. Entertaining, but I wouldn't count on it too much to help me if I were in real danger."

I was satisfied that this was all he had to show me. I was still sore at him for how he had reacted when Emily was in trouble. And perhaps, I also had not entirely forgotten the night he and Tracy spent in the tent two feet away from me. I got up, nodded coldly, and left. He didn't say anything. I don't think he had anything to say—Tessa one – Robbie nil.

Things move fast at Mark, and I realized that I had some hard goodbyes to say, and I'm the worst one for goodbyes. I get all emotional and teary, which I have to hide because it ruins my image in the world's eyes, so I get all bitchy and send people I love away hating me. But I didn't have a choice. The gang that had arrived at the island with me was scheduled to leave in three days, and I couldn't put it off any longer. I told Jamie to meet me on the beach after dinner. The resort has a lovely long private beach with nooks where you can sit in peace. When Jamie arrived, I guided him to the one farthest away from the path leading to the resort.

"You are leaving soon," I said. I left it hanging in the air.

"And you're not coming with us ..."

"No, I'm not, and I wanted us to be together tonight, only the two of us."

Jamie remained silent, gazing in the distance above my shoulder. I knew that I had to make it a clean-cut, that we would not see each other again, but sometimes I don't have the strength to do the right thing. Instead, I got closer and kissed him gently. After a while, he kissed me back. His eyes were moist.

"We didn't ... we didn't have the time to know each other. We didn't get a chance to see where this would go. We never even ..."

Had sex? I completed it for him, pushing the thought to him quickly. It's strange how, sometimes, it's easier to put a thought out there than to say it out loud. Jamie nodded, swallowed, and said nothing.

"Well, we can fix that," I said. "Come."

I got up. We were sitting on a boulder that ended in the sea, and I pulled him up after me. He followed me without saying a word, and I took him to my room. What a bittersweet evening that turned out to be!

The next evening I met with Tracy. It somehow didn't feel right to meet her on the same beach where I had met with her brother. I took her to the edge of the balcony, where I had had breakfast on the first morning. There was the entrance to an ancient stone building that looked like something that had helped fend pirates off in the distant past. It featured stone steps that took you to a turret. We climbed to the top and sat there, enjoying the breeze coming from the sea.

"I know you're deserting us," said Tracy, "and it sucks."

"It sucks indeed," I said, "but it's for the greater good."

"Greater good be screwed! I'll miss you like hell."

"I'll miss you too, and I want you to know how much."

"I believe you."

"I don't want you to believe me; I want you to know it. Do your thing."

Tracy gave me a surprised look, but then she nodded and came close. She put her hands on my waist and pulled me to her so our bodies touched. I had a flashback to that night in the crypt. It reminded me of the drunken feeling of sensing another beautiful human being melding with my inner soul. It all came rushing back to me. Then she kissed me like she had kissed me that night, and the world started to swirl around me. I don't know how long this went on. In my mind, I traveled at the speed of light through a beautiful tunnel of lights and colors. Eventually, she detached herself from me and took a half step back.

"I've seen it," she said simply.

"I've seen it too," I said, "and now I know we will be joined forever. There is a part of you dwelling in my soul now, and it will remain there until I die."

Tracy said nothing; she simply nodded in assent and caressed my cheek. We remained there until dawn, hugging on that turret and looking toward the horizon. And we no longer needed to speak.

Saying goodbye to the others was easier. I rode with them to the airport, and they stood before the airplane while I hugged them one by one. I had never liked Thomas very much, maybe because his first instinct when we had met was to suggest killing me. Also, he was the cause of Emily's death. Be that as it may, a simple "Bye" with a perfunctory hug was all he had earned.

I hadn't had an opportunity to get to know Sandie much, so she got the same treatment as Thomas, minus the hard feelings. Nolan was another story. I liked him, but you know, he was old—from my perspective, I mean, not really "old," just not ... young—so I gave him a daughterly hug. He kissed me on the cheek, which I thought was gross. I managed not to spoil the atmosphere by rubbing the kiss away, which is always my instinctive reaction to old people's kisses.

Tracy and Jamie embraced me together, murmuring words of affection that almost made me cry again. Jamie had tears in his eyes, and Tracy's lower lip was trembling as if she was about to cry too, so I thought it best to untangle before this got too cheesy. I took three steps back and lied out loud, "I'll be seeing you. I'll keep in touch, I promise," then I ran away and got into the car that had brought us there. From the darkened window, I saw them turning slowly, with bowed heads, and climb into the aircraft.

Since nobody was watching me, I had the luxury of wiping my eyes dry. I did it, and then I sat up straight. *Enough with this sappiness*, I said to myself. I had to get back to business. That orange dot on the screen, which was set to become red soon, was my first assignment, and I needed to prepare for it.

What was that orange dot about, you're asking? I won't tell you now; I'm too worn out and deserve a little rest before I plunge into the action again. You can read about it in my next report if you want.

What?

No, can't you take a hint? No previews! I need to be alone for a while.

Make an Author Happy Today

If you enjoyed **THE OTHERS** and wish to help me let more people know about it, please leave a review or a rating at your retailer.

Thank you!

Now read Chapter 1 of **HUNTER**, Book Three of the series.

HUNTER (BOOK 3) - CHAPTER 1 PREVIEW

Shooting pool all by yourself can be fun for a little while, but it gets boring in the end, and I had been doing it for two days in a row now. Boring! All I knew was that this was where the recruiter was likely to show up. I hoped that my platinum blond hair and my innocent blue eyes would be enticing enough for him to hit on me; otherwise, I would have to find another way to get in.

But wait a minute—you have no idea what this is all about, right? And you may be wondering what blond hair and blue eyes I'm blabbering about when you know very well that my hair is light brown and I have (beautiful, if you ask me) green eyes. I guess I'll better start from the beginning.

The last you heard from me, I had agreed to join Mission Ark (MARK to friends), that runs an operation from a lovely tiny island in the Canaries that shall remain nameless. MARK fights a bitter war against a shady organization secretly supported by some countries, which has a mission to find and kill every telepath on earth, me included. The island's facility is run by an unassuming middle-aged man named Jacob; he was the one who offered me a job.

That was two months ago, and since then, I had already been on a mission to save a telepath on which the killers were closing in. As you may know, telepaths tend to hide and distrust others; it comes from being a potential victim and the target of blind hate. That's why in this case, saving this telepath was uphill work. I found him quickly enough, but I had to work hard to convince him that he was in danger. I eventually managed to earn his trust and slip away with him before the assassins got to us, but it had been a close call. I took him to the island, where he would be given a new identity and a new place to live, some-where safer than before. We call that "recycling" here. When you are recycled, you get a new name and a new identity, as well as financial support to get you settled down in a new location. But that is not a permanent solution. It only means that you go back into hiding and try to live a reasonably good life until you must run away again. That's if you're lucky; the less lucky ones get killed.

Jacob was ecstatic that I had been successful on my first mission. He introduced me to Susan, who bore the somewhat vague title of "Head of Operations." MARK doesn't have a chain of command that is entirely clear to me, but perhaps that's on purpose.

Susan was a middle-aged woman, a bit overweight but not obese. She had black hair and matching black eyes that weren't cold but not warm either. She spoke slowly, as if each word had to pass inspection before leaving her mouth, and she had a slight accent that I could not place.

"I'm mad," was the first thing I told her as we met.

"What or who are you mad at?" she asked.

"I'm angry because all we do is run away. This may go on forever, us running and running and not getting anywhere. We're staying alive, but what kind of life is that?"

Susan smiled. The room in which we met had a beautiful wooden table with matching chairs. A teapot and cups were on the table. The china was thin, delicate, and obviously expensive, and it really looked as if it didn't belong there.

"Sit down, Tessa, and let me pour you some tea. You're preaching to the choir."

"What do you mean?"

I sat down, and Susan poured tea for me, taking time to answer. Jacob stood unobtrusively aside, sipping his tea while gazing out the window.

"You are exceptional, Tessa. You're powerful and experienced, and despite being so young, you already got yourself single-handedly out of life-threatening situations that most people would not survive. If our character analysis is right, which it usually is, the need to be proactive burns in you. You don't take adversities lying down; you confront them. That's why I think that you won't shy from danger if it's for the good of the cause. Am I right?"

"That is all very flattering, but it seems to me that you're about to tell me something I will not like. Why don't you stop beating about the bush and give it to me?"

Don't tell me I was being cheeky with my superior. First of all, I don't give a shit about ranks; I never did. And besides, that's who I am—a plain-speaking girl—and I like new people I meet to know that upfront.

"All right, let's cut to the chase, then," said Susan, nodding in assent. "We are escalating our war for survival. We no longer want to be passive and only run away; we want to be proactive."

"When you say, 'our war,' does that mean you're a telepath too? I know that Jacob is not one of us, and still, he works here."

"Why does that matter? Different people have different reasons for working with MARK."

"It matters because things are entirely different for a telepath than for a non-telepath. If you are a 'normal' person, you can return to your normal life when things go south. But for a telepath, there is no 'normal.' We are not running the same kind of risk, which is a factor I need to consider when I have to make decisions based on input from you."

"You're right, and you have the right to know. Yes, I am a telepath, but only a very weak one. I cannot control when telepathy happens ... but you could have checked that yourself."

"I have this stupid code I go by that forces me never to read someone who's on my side without permission."

"That's very commendable, and I appreciate it. Now let's go back to business."

"Let's," I agreed. I really wanted to know what she had in mind. If it was something more creative than running away all the time, I wanted to hear it. "But first, you said, 'we are escalating,' and I'd like to know who the 'we' to whom you refer are."

"MARK has a council established by people who support and fund us for various reasons. Some are closet telepaths, and others have family members who are. They are powerful people, and thank God for their support," Susan said. "Without them, MARK would not exist."

"Hmm, you can't be less specific than that, but it will do for now," I said.

"All right, let's go back to the point," said Susan. "It is true that the assassin's squads are sanctioned by governmental bodies, but to run them, they need lots of money, and that kind of funding cannot be hidden in government budgets without having questions asked. What happens is that big money doesn't come from the governments but from a few wealthy people who fund the operation. Those billionaires operating in different countries have come together to provide the money. They like to call themselves 'investors,' the bastards."

"But then, doesn't this make it even more difficult for us?" I wondered. "I was hoping that someone in government might investigate and put a stop to all this. But if the money doesn't come from the government, even if they decide to cut funds and close departments, the operation can go on privately."

"You're absolutely right, and that's why we need to go after the money. We don't know for sure, but we believe that the so-called 'investors' are only five, so if we can get rid of them and the funding goes away, we have won."

"Meaning that the plan is to find and kill them all?" I was excited at the prospect of doing something to end this nightmare but a bit less excited at the thought that I was apparently about to be asked to be an assassin again. I say "again" because it seems that people are always trying to convince me to use my powers to kill people, and somehow, I end up killing them, whether I like it or not (I usually don't). But I'm no killer; I've had to kill in self-defense, but I can't envision myself killing in cold blood. I'm weak in that sense, but that's how I like myself. I hope to have many years ahead of me, during which I will see myself in the mirror, and I want to like what I see there.

"Not necessarily," Susan said, brushing the question aside. "We need them neutralized whichever way. While I would have no qualms about killing each of them with my bare hands, it may be better for us to come up with other options. Some of them may be involved in shady businesses, which can end them in jail. There may also be other ways of handling them, like ruining their business, so they no longer have the money to fund the operation."

"What would I have to do?"

"As I said, we need to hunt them down and neutralize them one by one. That involves executing some pretty complex and dangerous plans, and I don't know in all of MARK anyone better qualified for that than you. But as I said, that kind of work is dangerous."

My excitement was growing. That was the stuff that I wanted to do. It was my opportunity to do something positive that might resolve our situation and give me a future to look forward to. The vision of a time when I could go back home and meet family and friends flashed before my eyes. I blinked to make it disappear;

letting your wishful thinking meld with reality never pays. Still, I was entirely on board with working toward that ideal future.

"The hunted becomes the hunter. I like that. Screw the danger! Tell me what to do," I said.

"I knew it," said Jacob with his low, musical voice. I had almost forgotten that he was there. I turned to look at him and found him smiling a broad smile at me.

NOTE ON THE TROXLER EFFECT

In Chapter 10, Tracy turns into a marble cherub for a few seconds. Well, that's not a hundred percent fantasy. Strange changes in what we see and the apparition of non-existent faces in the mirror are attributable to the Troxler Effect.

Troxler's fading, also known as the Troxler Effect, is an optical illusion affecting visual perception. When one fixates on a particular point for even a short period, an unchanging stimulus away from the fixation point will fade away and disappear. Recent research suggests that at least some portion of the perceptual phenomena associated with Troxler's fading occurs in the brain. Since, in our story, Tracy projects stimuli directly to the viewer's mind, she can turn herself into a cherub in the eye of the beholder.

Troxler's fading has been attributed to the adaptation of neurons vital for perceiving stimuli in the visual system. It is part of the general principle in sensory systems that unvarying stimuli soon disappear from our awareness.

On the next page, I have included an image. If you gaze at a high-resolution version of the image for a few seconds, concentrating your eyes on the cross, you will see the colors disappear, and the image turn light gray. If you view a grayscale version of the

171

image instead, you will still note the effect, but not as clearly as in color. This is a demonstration of the Troxler Effect. If you can't see this image in high resolution, just google "Troxler Effect" to find it.

You can read more about it in a paper by Prof. Giovanni B. Caputo. Just google "Strange face in the mirror illusion."

Have fun with it.

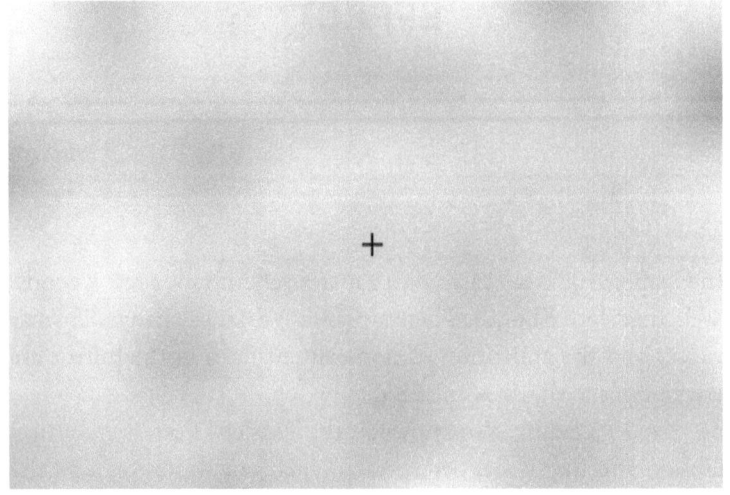

MEET THE AUTHOR

Kfir Luzzatto is the author of thirteen novels, several short stories, and seven non-fiction books. Kfir was born and raised in Italy and moved to Israel as a teenager. He acquired the love for the English language from his father, a former U.S. soldier, a voracious reader, and a prolific writer. Kfir has a Ph.D. in chemical engineering and works as a patent attorney. He lives in Omer, Israel, with his full-time partner, Esther, their four children, Michal, Lilach, Tamar, and Yonatan, and the dog Elvis.

In pursuit of his interest in the mind-body connection, Kfir was certified as a Clinical Hypnotherapist by the Anglo European College of Therapeutic Hypnosis.

Kfir has published extensively in the professional and general press over the years. For almost four years, he wrote a weekly "Patents" column in Globes (Israel's financial newspaper). His popular guide, *FUN WITH PATENTS—The Irreverent Guide for the Investor, the Entrepreneur, and the Inventor*, was published in 2016. He is an HWA (Horror Writers Association) and ITW (International Thriller Writers) member.

You can visit Kfir's website and read his blog at www.kfirluzzatto.com. Follow him on Twitter (@KfirLuzzatto) and friend him on Facebook (https://www.facebook.com/ Kfir-LuzzattoAuthor/).

ALSO BY KFIR LUZZATTO:

CROSSING THE MEADOW

THE ODYSSEY GENE

THE EVELYN PROJECT

HAVE BOOK, WILL TRAVEL
(With Yonatan Luzzatto)

AN ITALIAN OBSESSION

EXODUS '95

CHIPLESS

REWIRED (*The sequel to CHIPLESS*)

ONCE AWAKENED

The Tessa Extra-Sensory Agent series:

TESSA (Tessa Extra-Sensory Agent Book 1)

THE OTHERS (Tessa Extra-Sensory Agent Book 2)

HUNTER (Tessa Extra-Sensory Agent Book 3)

PHANTOM (Tessa Extra-Sensory Agent Book 4)

RUNNER (Tessa Extra-Sensory Agent Book 5)

The DEAD & BUSY series:

#1: ACCIDENTAL LAZARUS

#2: PHANTOM LOVER

#3: MICE

#4: THE ACCOUNTANT

Short Story Collections:

HIS DARKER SIDE

HIS LIGHTER SIDE